KU-401-707

# ROBERT MUCHAMORE'S
# ROBIN HOOD

## RANSOMS, RAIDS & REVENGE

HOT
KEY
BOOKS

First published in Great Britain in 2022 by
HOT KEY BOOKS
4th Floor, Victoria House, Bloomsbury Square
London WC1B 4DA
Owned by Bonnier Books
Sveavägen 56, Stockholm, Sweden
www.hotkeybooks.com

Copyright © Robert Muchamore, 2022

All rights reserved.
No part of this publication may be reproduced, stored or transmitted
in any form or by any means, electronic, mechanical, photocopying or
otherwise, without the prior written permission of the publisher.

The right of Robert Muchamore to be identified as author of this work has
been asserted by them in accordance with the Copyright, Designs and
Patents Act 1988.

This is a work of fiction. Names, places, events and incidents are either the
products of the author's imagination or used fictitiously. Any resemblance
to actual persons, living or dead, is purely coincidental.

A CIP catalogue record for this book is available from the British Library.

ISBN: 978-1-4714-1231-8
*Also available as an ebook and in audio*

1

Typeset by DataConnection Ltd
Printed and bound in Great Britain by Clays Ltd, Elcograf S.p.A.

Hot Key Books is an imprint of Bonnier Books UK
www.bonnierbooks.co.uk

# ROBIN HOOD

# THE STORY SO FAR . . .

**The bad guys are scheming . . .**

For more than a decade, **Guy Gisborne** has used threats, violence and corruption to keep the declining industrial town of Locksley under his thumb. Now he wants to expand his influence across the whole county by becoming Sheriff of Nottingham.

Outgoing Sheriff **Marjorie Kovacevic** has even grander plans. She's entered the race to become national president and is ahead of her rivals in the latest polls.

Election day is less than six months away. If the pair win power, they'll be unstoppable in their quest to smash the rebels in Sherwood Forest.

**While the good guys struggle . . .**

After the destruction of their base in a devastating fire, rebel leader **Will Scarlock** is trying to establish new headquarters inside the luxurious but flood-damaged Sherwood Castle Resort.

Thirteen-year-old **Robin Hood** and the other Sherwood Forest rebels want a better society, where everyone gets quality education, housing and healthcare – and crooks like Guy Gisborne get a prison uniform instead of a sheriff's badge. But with temperatures below freezing and the forest blanketed in snow, the fight for justice must take a back seat as the rebels struggle to find the food, fuel and medicines they need just to stay alive.

# 1. TEN MAN ERIC

Robin Hood stumbled. The deep snow meant he never quite knew when his boot would hit solid ground, making it easy to stub a toe on a hidden rock or twist an ankle stepping awkwardly on tree roots.

'Looks like a storm drain,' Robin told the other three members of the search party as he probed around, stabbing his walking pole into the snow. 'It's not deep, but mind your step.'

Two plumes of breath curled out of Robin's nose and up towards the dazzling cloudless sky. It had been a tough two-hour trek. His fingers and face were numb. While Robin was breathless enough to gulp air through his mouth, he fought the urge because frosty air sent sharp pains through his teeth.

Robin's three companions were well insulated. Ten-year-old Matt Maid wore tatty pink ski pants and a hooded parka jacket. He'd moaned before they left, saying the trousers were too bulky, but now he was grateful his mum had insisted, because they were super warm and repelled water better than Robin's sodden combat trousers.

Rebel security officer Lyla Masri led the way down into the drainage channel, while Ten Man Eric brought up the rear. Ten Man was a powerfully built German, with crude prison tattoos on his cheek and neck. He'd spent half his fifty years behind bars and earned his nickname because they said it took ten men to bring him down in a fight.

Lyla, reaching out with her walking pole, found a set of steps on the opposite side of the trench. Robin joined her, then stepped onto a low wall to get a view over a huge snow-covered car park and the burnt remains of Sherwood Designer Outlets.

The vast mall had been abandoned for over a decade, before becoming Will Scarlock's rebel headquarters. A few months earlier Sheriff Marjorie's helicopters had dropped incendiaries across the roof; now all that remained of the rebels' base was a snow-blanketed tangle of collapsed walls, melted beams and blackened interior fixtures.

'Someone's got a fire going,' Matt said, pointing to wispy smoke over the far side of the mall, near a frozen stretch of the Macondo River.

Lyla gave the rifle slung over her shoulder a reassuring tap. 'We heard there's bandits in the area. Hopefully they won't bother us if we don't bother them.'

Ten Man grunted, as if to say *I'll believe that when I see it.*

The quartet's equipment packs rattled as they jogged across one of the huge parking lots encircling the burnt-out mall. There was soot beneath the snow, which squelched underfoot and sprayed dark grey slush up Robin's trousers.

They stumbled over chunks of a fallen wall, and soon they were beneath the sagging metal frame that had once supported the mall's glass-domed atrium. Pebbles of shatterproof glass crunched underfoot. Although the air was below freezing, sunlight was melting snow on the metal frame, making an eerie chorus of drips.

Their target was on the far side of the atrium, where a football-pitch-sized area of charred wood and melted plastic roofing had cascaded down in a heap. It peaked at ten metres and had solidified into a huge lump as it cooled.

Ten Man squatted and began to take equipment out of his enormous backpack. Matt stared ruefully up at the snow-covered remains of the first-floor food court, where he'd spent hundreds of hours riding his skateboard and hanging with his crew.

'Sad to see it in this state,' Ten Man told Matt, in a voice too soft for his heavy physique and prison tattoos. 'Were you born in here?'

Matt shook his head. 'We came when I was a toddler, but all my memories are here.'

Ten Man had started work in a German coal mine aged sixteen, but quickly realised it was no fun. At eighteen, he stole a truck filled with mining explosives and used his tunnelling skills to rob banks and high-end watch stores all over Europe.

The robberies had been a success, but a youthful appetite for lavish spending and fast cars meant that Ten Man caught police attention – and prison time – in four countries. After escaping to Sherwood Forest, he'd become one of Will Scarlock's most trusted people. Tough enough to make opponents back off without a fight, smart enough to be more than just muscle, and well liked, despite his scary nickname.

After a quick break, sharing cheese sandwiches and a warming flask of spicy noodle soup, the quartet got to work. Lyla climbed the skeletal remains of an escalator to stand guard from the first floor, while Ten Man and the two boys approached the mountain of collapsed roof wearing headlamps on elastic straps and carrying axes, metal detectors and battery-powered saws.

Rebel search parties had retrieved possessions and valuables from the mall after the fire, but locating valuable items trapped below tonnes of melted roofing seemed impossible, until Ten Man had the idea of using a stash of mining gear that he'd previously employed to burrow into a Berlin gold depository and Capital City's swankiest jewellery store.

Since they were after stuff from Will Scarlock's command tent, Ten Man clambered gingerly onto the part of the molten roof that was closest to the protruding beams from the watchtower. He was worried about ice, and the chance that debris might shift when he put his weight down. But the molten resin had set hard and the mound felt solid.

As Ten Man walked, he swept a long-handled sonar probe over the wreckage. The ancient German device had a flickering green display, but a skilled operator could interpret the blurry lines as sand, clay, rock or even a gas-filled cavity that would blow you to bits if your cutting tool made a spark.

Robin and Matt kept close behind until Ten Man saw something he liked on the screen. He went down on one knee, got a squeal from a little handheld metal detector, then used a hand axe to make a fist-sized hole.

'What are you seeing?' Robin asked.

'Something metal,' Ten Man told him before moving on. 'Let me know when you figure it out.'

As Matt trailed Ten Man over the tangle of wood and roofing, Robin kicked away as much snow as he could before lying on his belly in front of the hole Ten Man had made. He switched on his headlamp and looked down, but the hole was too small for him to see anything, so he took the battery-powered hand saw off his belt and set to work.

When the hole was the size of a dinner plate, Robin stuck his head in. His headlamp shone over a cavity the size of a small car, and he inhaled soot that tickled his nose and made him sneeze.

After wiping snot off his top lip, Robin held his breath as he went down for a second look. It seemed the metal

Ten Man had detected was a buckled scaffold pole that had once supported Will's command tent. Robin also recognised a run of brightly coloured cables that once fed data between the mall's internet router and a satellite dish atop the watchtower.

'We're definitely in the right area,' Robin announced.

He got no response, because Matt was noisily sawing another hole a dozen metres away. And this time Ten Man was excited enough to stand and watch.

'It's big and rectangular,' Ten Man told Matt excitedly as he studied a bright spot on his scanner screen. 'Exactly what we came for.'

Robin wanted to clamber over and join the excitement, but the soot had really done him in and he had to pause while the next sneeze built in his nose.

He sneezed twice. When he looked up after a third, a big-eyed child said, 'Bless you.'

Robin was startled by the small sturdy girl, standing on the debris less than two metres away. She was no older than six, with matted hair and a soot-blackened face. Lyla hadn't spotted her approach, and Robin realised she wasn't wearing enough winter clothes to be more than playing distance from home.

He decided to grab the girl and find where she'd come from, but she gasped and hurtled back down the mound before he could get close. At the same moment, Ten Man noisily stamped out a section of charred roofing that Matt had cut along three sides.

'This is it,' Matt said, excitedly as his headlamp flickered inside the new hole. 'I can see Will Scarlock's safe!'

Robin grinned and gasped. On the night Sherwood Designer Outlets had burned, the safe had crashed through the melting roof. It contained over £80,000 that the rebels desperately needed to buy supplies, and £7,800 that was Robin's remaining share of the loot from a cash machine robbery he'd masterminded back in the spring.

# 2. SCRUMPING TRUCKS

TwoTu – short for The World to You – had started twenty-five years earlier with a website selling second-hand air conditioners and hotel furniture out of a warehouse in Tshwane, South Africa.

Now TwoTu's founder, Rex Lairde, was one of the world's richest men. His company had vast robot-operated distribution warehouses on five continents and a half a million garish green vans offering next-day delivery on everything from frozen chicken curry to six-seat sofas.

Irene Clarke's TwoTu van was one of the sleek electric ones they showed in the latest social media ads. She didn't love the delivery job, but she knew that a sixty-year-old ex-con in a grotty town like Locksley was lucky to have any job at all.

Delivering to New World Apartments was a pain, because the building had eleven floors and there was always a good chance that the rattly piss-stinking elevators would be out of order.

The rectangular screen strapped on Irene's wrist displayed her next customer's name and delivery address as she parked. As she stepped into the van's rear compartment, it told her to grab two carrier bags from Bay 78 and three from the refrigerated compartment. It also began a countdown. If she didn't make the delivery in one minute and forty-six seconds, the device would flash red and vibrate, telling her she was falling behind schedule.

Frosty air hit Irene's green TwoTu fleece and her foot slipped as she stepped onto the kerb holding five bulging grocery bags. Her wrist unit counted down eight more seconds as she reached a battered metal door and scanned an intercom panel to find the button for Apartment 714.

'Seventh floor,' a lad said cheerfully before buzzing her in.

Irene reckoned the bags stuffed with beer, snacks and ready meals were for uni students. The lift was waiting inside a damp lobby full of chained-up bikes and buggies. She'd heard stories about people getting stuck in elevators and Locksley Housing not coming out to rescue them for days, but her only other option was fourteen flights of stairs.

As the elevator's door squealed closed and the lift started to move, Irene's wrist unit automatically sent a signal to lock the van. But it didn't lock, because thirteen-year-old Marion Maid stood shivering near the exit of

New World Apartments' trash chute, and the pocket of her thick winter jacket contained a jamming device that blocked the signal.

'Driver is in the lift,' eighteen-year-old goth Neo Scarlock told Marion as the two rebels exited the building through a broken fire door. 'Let's get to work.'

The pair wore vinyl gloves to prevent fingerprints, and pulled up their hoodies as they moved off, because TwoTu's electric vehicles came with an eight-camera sentry system.

'Easy-peasy, lemon squeezy,' Neo said cheerfully as the driver's door slid open. He let Marion step inside before taking the driver's seat. 'Does my Padawan remember what I taught her last night?'

'Mostly,' Marion said anxiously as she knelt in the footwell in front of the flip-up passenger seat and located a rubber bung over an OBD2 port. This is a required feature in the footwell of all road vehicles, enabling fire crews and roadside assistance to diagnose faults and access key systems.

Marion plugged a battered smartphone into the socket.

'Open the app and enter the reboot code,' Neo instructed. 'Then upload our special sauce.'

'Hash-nine-one-one-hash,' Marion mouthed to herself.

'Rewrite Operating System is the third menu,' Neo said impatiently as Marion scrolled.

'I know,' she growled back.

Neo glanced in the back of the van as the software began to upload through the port. 'Van's full of packages. Must have caught the driver on one of her first deliveries.'

As Neo looked back, the lights inside the van died, the refrigerator's compressor stopped whirring, and the dashboard display turned black.

During the development of TwoTu's electric vans, a disgruntled engineer had leaked security details. Hackers then wrote software that could be uploaded through the OBD2 and let anyone drive off – without needing a connection to a delivery driver's wrist unit.

Fifty seconds after Marion's upload, the van's dashboard display rebooted, but TwoTu's corporate logo had been replaced by a skull and the sound system celebrated the triumphant hack with a jaunty rendition of 'The Sailor's Hornpipe'.

'All mine!' Neo said exuberantly, then complimented Marion. 'Nice job.'

Marion sat in the flip-up passenger seat, Neo hit the accelerator pedal, and by the time Irene Clarke exited New World Apartments and realised her van had been stolen, the two teenage rebels were out of sight.

# 3. KENTUCKY FRIED HINGES

Matt was the lightest member of the search party, but he wasn't keen to be lowered into a soot-filled hole, so Robin put on a respirator mask while Ten Man expertly used neon parachute cord to tie a Swiss-seat harness around Robin's waist and thighs.

'No sign of that little girl,' Lyla called from her observation post on the first floor. 'And no life in the parking lots.'

'They're out there,' Ten Man called back warily, connecting Robin's harness to a rope. 'Kid that young can't be alone.'

Robin fought off another sneeze as he sat with his legs dangling through the hole. The safe was wedged in a tangle of debris eight metres down, beams and planks crisscrossing the drop.

Ten Man let the rope attached to Robin glide through his gloved hands as the teenager pushed off the edge and into the hole.

'Drop me another metre,' Robin said, as he dangled in the dark.

As Ten Man steadily lowered the rope, Robin's boots hit some beams blocking his way to the bottom. Kicking didn't shift them, so Robin tipped himself forward in the harness and used his electric saw, cutting a V-shape out of a beam so that it was weak enough to snap with a kick.

'Looks clear to the bottom now,' Robin shouted up.

When the teenager touched down on the pinkish tiles of the atrium floor he glanced at the safe, then flinched as a pulley line landed by him, almost whacking him in the face.

Robin pulled the line tight and tied it off on a beam, so they could safely lower equipment. The enclosed space made his breathing seem loud, and when he looked up it was like a church steeple, with sunlight piercing the rough rectangular hole at the top.

The first thing Ten Man sent down was a work lamp with a couple of hundred LEDs. Robin pointed it at Will Scarlock's safe and squinted as his eyes adjusted to the dazzle.

'What you seeing?' Ten Man shouted.

The safe's exterior was blackened, and one side had buckled in the fire. The rectangular cabinet was waist-high and looked hefty, but it was a medium-security office safe designed to secure papers or valuables, rather than the heavily armoured monsters Ten Man had blasted open in banks and jewellers.

'Seems intact,' Robin said. As he got closer, he noticed finger-marks in the soot around the safe's handle and electronic keypad. 'But I'm not the first person to come down here . . .'

After adjusting part of the rope harness, which kept riding up his bum crack, Robin walked to the back of the safe. As a drip of water hit his nose, he studied the area where three door hinges joined the heavy case.

The dark grey enamel finish had silver swirls where someone had attacked it with an angle grinder. Where the door hinges met the body of the safe there were deeper gouges, and the door didn't seem to be on straight.

'I'll secure the big pulley, then we can haul it up,' Ten Man shouted. 'You'll have to saw a couple more beams.'

Robin was only half listening as he grabbed the safe's metal handle. His fears were confirmed as the door rocked and made a hollow clank.

'Someone beat us to it,' Robin shouted up, leaning back to wrench open the heavy door.

The door slid open faster than expected; it would have smashed Robin's toes if he hadn't jumped back. A corner of the heavy door hit the floor, cracking a tile and causing enough vibration to raise specks of soot, that caught the beam from the work lamp.

'OK down there?' Ten Man asked.

'It's a bust.' Robin groaned as he stared into the safe.

Instead of Robin's life savings and the rebels' cash reserves, there were scorch marks and dead spiders.

'Are you sure?' Matt asked incredulously.

Robin sounded irritated. 'Come look yourself if you don't believe me.'

Ten Man swore under his breath. 'Any sign how they got down there?'

Robin was already wondering about this, and shone the work lamp around. Daylight was seeping through one corner of the cavern close to floor level. When Robin squatted, he could see a tunnel that had been hacked through the debris. It was a couple of metres long and broad enough for a teen or slim adult to crawl through.

Robin's disappointment began to sink in: the snowy two-hour trek to get back, the risks he'd taken to steal the money from the cash machine in the first place, his shattered dreams of the replacement laptop and new boots he'd hoped to spend his money on.

'I'll pull you up,' Ten Man told Robin, then looked at Matt. 'Take the gear and start packing up.'

Robin was three metres up and navigating past the beam he'd sawed when he heard a sharp crack from above. The sound was muffled by the layers of debris, but Robin knew a gunshot when he heard one. Then, as he dangled helplessly, he heard gruff shouts, the barking of dogs, and Lyla yelling.

'What's going on?' he shouted warily.

Ten Man gave no answer, because he was using his massive strength to pull the rope and get Robin out of the cavern ASAP. The thirteen-year-old had his arms up, ready to grab the sides of the hole, when the rope jerked, dropping him two metres.

Robin saw a shadow step across the hole. Ten Man roared and thumped someone. Robin heard a body thud on the burnt roofing, then his rope made a zipping sound as he fell fast. He tried to grip a metal pole, but crashed into it instead.

The sleeve of Robin's coat ripped on jagged debris. His head jerked back, but the tearing fabric had slowed him enough to save him from a hard landing. Ten Man was still having a punch-up overhead as Robin detached his harness from the pile of rope that had landed beside him and began a rapid crawl through sooty puddles to the light creeping into the far corner.

Robin's respirator had been knocked askew when he landed, so he breathed in all the dust he'd disturbed. He had no idea how far the gap in the debris went, or where it exited, but he had no other option.

After crawling several metres over the mall floor, the tunnel took a sharp turn. The light got brighter, and Robin was relieved to see that he could exit over a sheet of roofing. He emerged, blinking and coughing, then something jumped onto his back. He was face down on a pile of debris before he'd taken a step.

A huge slobbering Doberman sank its teeth into Robin's wrist before a woman in a grubby pink fur coat yelled, 'Good boy!' and grabbed its collar to pull the muscular dog back.

Thick clothing meant the bite barely broke Robin's skin, but before he could work out what was happening, he got a ferocious kick in the thigh, which gave him a dead leg. The woman with the dog yanked Robin to his feet, while a kid of about sixteen with dirt-encrusted dreadlocks tugged Robin's respirator mask, stretched the elastic straps as far as they'd go, then sadistically let it ping back in his face.

The powerful dog reared up, the woman twisted Robin's wrist up behind his back, and the youth pulled a hunting knife crusted in dry blood and swooshed it below his chin.

'Robin Hood,' the youth said, giving a smile that revealed a single brown stump where his lower front teeth should be. 'There's a nice juicy bounty on your head!'

# 4. TWOTU TEAR-DOWN

Marion's nerves jangled as the stolen TwoTu truck took a ramp onto a deserted four-lane highway, passing a battered Locksley Police Department cruiser with two officers standing in front wearing shades. One held a radar speed gun, while her partner tucked into food from Mindy Burger. The yellow bags of fries and onion rings had been torn open and spread across the hood of the cruiser.

If they'd been inside their cruiser, the cops would have seen the automatic numberplate recognition system flash red as it scanned the plate of a TwoTu van that had been reported stolen six minutes earlier. If the cop with the radar gun hadn't been dunking curly fries into mayo, she might even have noticed that there were two scruffy forest kids riding in the TwoTu van rather than one green-uniformed driver.

But when Neo looked in his side mirror, there was no sign of the cops starting a chase. Marion cracked a wry smile.

'Brown underwear moment,' she quipped.

Eleven minutes later, they took an off-ramp at the junction with Old Road. This winding route through Sherwood Forest hadn't officially reopened after being damaged in the summer floods, and they saw no other traffic until they drove onto the overgrown lot of a motel that hadn't seen a paying guest in thirty years.

They stopped behind a row of snow-capped wooden lodges that looked ready to cave in. Neo's older brother, Sam, raced towards the truck as Marion jumped out into the snow.

'Any bother?' Sam asked, banging his gloved hands together to keep warm.

Neo shrugged and pulled an *are you stupid?* face at his big brother. 'We're here, ain't we?'

Marion looked around at a chaotic scene. At its heart were two more bright green TwoTu vans. One had arrived fifteen minutes earlier, and a crew of scruffy rebels were unpacking the cargo from the rear, opening cardboard TwoTu packages.

The second truck had been stolen several hours earlier. Its cargo was long gone, it had been jacked up, and a crew of three rebels and two members of the Brigands Motorcycle Club were stripping it for parts.

The rebels got dibs on the van's battery packs, which they would repurpose as part of Will Scarlock's grand plan to give his new Sherwood Castle headquarters a reliable electricity supply. The bearded Brigands were professional vehicle thieves. While TwoTu's vans were custom built and too distinctive to be sold on as complete vehicles, each contained thousands of pounds' worth of standard parts, from tyres to wiper motors, that could be stripped out and sold to repair shops.

'Not the greenest scene I've ever seen,' Marion said to nobody in particular, thinking about nearly new vehicles being trashed for a few hundred pounds' worth of parts, and watching soggy TwoTu cardboard boxes blowing in the snow. She found a wooden porch where one of the Brigands' wives was serving hot tea, rum punch and hot dogs to keep everyone going in the freezing conditions. Marion pulled off her thick gloves to add ketchup and chopped onions to her dog, but had barely taken her second bite when Neo told her to eat fast and help with unloading.

They took bags of refrigerated food out of the van first, then half a dozen rebels got to work unloading and opening stacks of brown TwoTu packages. It was cold but fun, because each box was a lucky dip and people laughed or clapped if they found something decent.

Sam Scarlock told Marion she was a good luck charm when the first box she opened contained boxes of tampons, which were always in short supply in the forest. A big laugh went up when someone opened a box containing fake blood and six comedy wigs, and Marion set a big purple afro wig on her head as she opened and sorted boxes of books, drills, Lego, ink cartridges and a laundry airer.

Food and anything else useful was loaded in a Land Rover that would be driven to Sherwood Castle. Stuff worth reselling went into a van and would be sold to a trader in Nottingham, while junk like cheap plastic clocks and novelty beer mats that were of too little value to resell were dumped in one of the abandoned motel lodges.

By the time the truck Neo and Marion stole had been emptied, a fourth stolen TwoTu van had arrived. But when Marion lined up at the back doors to help empty it, Neo called her over.

'The car with all the fresh food is about to leave for the castle,' he explained. 'You'll be squashed, but there's space for you in the back.'     –

It was super cold, but Marion liked bantering with the crew and opening boxes so she shook her head. 'The more people here, the faster we get the job done,' she argued.

Neo laughed. 'Your mums said I could take you as long as you only had the *morning* off school. If you leave now, you should make afternoon lessons.'

'I thought we were a team,' Marion pleaded, aiming for Neo's sense of cool. 'Don't be a dork.'

Neo rolled his eyes and made Marion flinch by acting like he was going to flick the end of her nose. 'This *dork* doesn't want earache from Karma and Indio. And if you don't get back on time, they'll never let you out to steal another truck.'

Marion tutted and kicked up a cloud of snow. Neo was right, but she didn't want to admit it so she stomped over to the waiting Land Rover.

She rode back to Sherwood Castle in her purple wig, squashed against desperately needed supplies stolen from the world's second biggest online retailer. The gear included winter coats, mobile phones, duvets, baby formula and a monstrous pack of toilet rolls that the driver wedged onto Marion's lap before slamming the back door.

# 5. WHAT WOULD ROBIN DO?

Matt Maid was a skinny ten-year-old who liked to talk big. But while achievements on a skateboard or playing *Call of Duty* might impress his mates, Matt now had to make grown-up decisions.

It was pure luck that Matt had missed the bandits' ambush. Ten Man had asked him to start clearing up the equipment. A length of rope had slipped off Matt's shoulder when he jumped off the debris mound, and he was on one knee coiling it back up when the four bandits jumped Ten Man.

As Matt crawled away, he saw two more bandits ambush Lyla and poke a rifle between her shoulder blades. When the powerful dog knocked Robin down, Matt felt sure that someone would grab him from behind or aim a gun at him and order him to freeze. But one minute later Matt sat breathlessly on the snowy tiles, his back against the low concrete wall around the atrium's fountain.

As he brushed beads of shatterproof glass off his padded trousers, his first thought was to phone for help. But few spots in the forest had a signal, so it was no surprise when he peeked at the phone inside his jacket and saw a red X on the signal bar.

Matt's next idea was to run. He'd lived in the forest his whole life, and while he'd never been this far from home on his own, he was confident that he'd be able to navigate back to Sherwood Castle. But it would take two hours, and then he'd have to explain what had happened and come back with a rescue team. By which time Robin, Lyla and Ten Man would be long gone.

*I can't abandon them*, Matt thought. *What would Robin do?*

Thinking about Robin dented Matt's confidence. It wasn't just that Robin was older, or a fearless climber, or a better shot with a bow and arrow. Robin had a special aura. Most kids froze when things got dangerous, but that's when Robin thrived.

*I'm not Robin.*

*I can't fix this.*

*I still climb into Mum's bed when I have a nightmare.*

A deep male roar boomed in the distance. Matt peeked over the concrete wall and saw that Ten Man had tried to break loose of his four captors. The mean dog started to bark and the woman with the rifle – the one who'd captured Lyla – closed in and aimed the gun at Ten Man's chest.

'I'll blow your head off!' she shouted. 'You ain't worth nothing.'

Seeing the woman point the gun made Matt consider his enemy. The bandits were filthy and raggedly dressed. He'd escaped, which meant their ambush was poorly planned. And why would they send four guys to wrestle Ten Man when they could have just pointed a gun at him?

*Because they only have one gun . . . Two, now they've taken Lyla's rifle . . .*

Matt felt a touch more confident as he watched the eight bandits, three captives and one mean dog exit through the remains of the mall's main entrance, then head across the south parking lot towards a riverside camp and the smoking fire he'd spotted when they arrived.

He was outnumbered and his only weapon was a little utility knife, but Matt felt sure he was facing lightly armed bandits who'd got lucky, rather than an elite crew dispatched to claim the bounty on Robin's head.

*I can do this*, Matt told himself as he stood up. *I may not be Robin Hood, but I'm not stupid and I've got surprise on my side.*

*But what exactly should I do?*

After glancing around, Matt hopped over the fountain wall and made a crouching run back towards the debris mound. The bandit crew had grabbed the equipment around the hole, including Matt's own backpack and Robin's bow, but they hadn't bothered with Ten Man's extra-large pack.

It was too heavy for Matt to lift, so he dragged it to a less open spot and rummaged through it. There was no sign of the gun he'd hoped to find, but he took a bigger knife, a canteen of water, a small pair of binoculars and a lighter.

His pockets bulged and the binoculars swung around Matt's neck as he set off towards the bandit camp. After a flat-out sprint across the exposed parking lot, he reached a long earth levee built to stop floodwater from reaching the mall.

He lay at the top of the snowy, sloping embankment and raised the binoculars to his eyes. The bandit camp was a fragile affair, set way too close to the stream. Three shacks had been built from plastic sheeting and debris from the mall. There was fishing gear with lines in the icy water, a tatty open-hulled motorboat, a pair of red gas cylinders and the large smoking fire.

Around the fire was well-trodden ground where snow and mud had been trampled into a slushy mess. Ten Man and Lyla had been ordered to sit cross-legged in this dirt, guarded by a jittery middle-aged man, who seemed to have rushed out of bed before putting his outdoor clothes on.

Matt eyed the backpacks and gear on the ground near the fire, including his own pack and Robin's bow. In another sign of the bandits' lack of organisation, Ten Man seemed free to move his arms around, and while Matt's view of Lyla was obscured, he felt sure she wasn't tied up either.

While the adult captives were being ignored, Robin was getting all the attention. He was twenty metres from the fire, surrounded by excited bandits who made him kneel, his hands behind his head. While the older bandits huddled up, discussing their next step, three grubby lads in their late teens tormented Robin, posing for selfies and making threats.

Matt couldn't hear every word, but one lad had sliced a clump of hair from the back of Robin's head and was making a joke about selling it online to the young hero's admirers.

'We'd make more if we cut off his ear,' another joked, before putting his boot against Robin's back and knocking him face first into the icy dirt.

'Don't break him – he's worth money,' an older woman shouted from the huddle.

'Dirtbags,' Matt muttered, feeling more determined than scared as one lad yanked Robin up by the back of his hoodie and laughed at the muddy snow streaking down his face.

# 6. COOKING WITH GAS

With all but one bandit focused on Robin, Matt reckoned he should help Ten Man and Lyla. The ten-year-old knew he had no chance if he attacked head on, so he figured his best shot was to distract their single nervous guard and give them a chance to break loose.

*But what if I'm wrong?*

*What if Robin gets killed?*

*What if . . . ?*

*Maybe I should run and get help.*

Matt gulped, then stood up and tried to imagine himself as a hero.

*I can be like Robin. He's not superhuman . . .*

Matt clambered over the top of the levee and kept low as he scrambled through trees and bushes towards the tents on the riverbank. The snow crunching and branches cracking under his boots sounded loud to him, but nobody seemed to hear as he reached the riverbank mud, which had a delicate sheet of ice on top.

He'd seen no sign of life inside the tents through the binoculars, but Matt's nerves still jangled as he approached the shack at the far edge. It was the largest of the three and he squelched cautiously towards the back.

A rubber hose ran in from the red gas bottle outside the tent. Matt peered through the semi-translucent plastic sheeting to make sure nobody was inside, then made a slash with his knife and reached through.

The gas bottle was linked to a knee-height camping stove, with a heater at the front and two cooking rings on top. He pulled the rubber hose from the back of the stove and was pleased with the gentle hissing sound and whiff of gas.

Cooking-gas fires were a hazard of forest life, and one of the strongest commandments of Matt's early childhood had been to never-never-never touch or even go near a gas appliance. But he'd also witnessed a posse who'd been trying to capture Robin using a gas explosion as a very effective distraction . . .

As Matt waited nervously, wondering if the gas he could smell was poisonous and unsure how much would have to build up inside the tent to make a decent explosion, he could hear the bandits arguing about the best way to claim Robin's bounty.

Guy Gisborne had offered £250,000 to anyone who brought Robin Hood to him alive. But the gangster was notoriously untrustworthy and tight with money.

'Seriously think Gisborne's gonna pay a quarter million to you no-hopers?' Robin taunted. 'He'd sooner chop you up and feed you to his pigs.'

This earned Robin a crack around the head from one of the youths, and a warning to shut his face.

Matt had backed away from the shack, but the smell of gas was getting stronger. The bandits would surely smell it soon too. A thousand warnings from both of Matt's mothers ran through his brain as he pulled Ten Man's lighter from his pocket.

Squatting behind a rock, Matt read a reassuring sticker on the lighter that said it was *guaranteed wind-resistant*. Matt couldn't help his hand trembling as he flung the lit lighter towards the hole he'd cut in the plastic.

Before he could lower his head, a huge fireball shot up through the surrounding trees and the shack's plastic skin vaporised. A screaming pregnant woman ran out of the furthest shack as its plastic roof turned to string cheese in the heat, but Matt had no time to pity her.

The backpacks were by the fire, less than ten metres from Matt. He squinted in the heat and glare as he ran. As he'd hoped, Ten Man used the blast as an opportunity to wrap his arms around his guard and drive him head first into the frozen ground.

Lyla grabbed a chunk of wood to use as a weapon. As the bandits looked confused, Matt snatched up the pack with Robin's bow inside and kept running until he reached a line of bushes. There was a shattering bang behind him as the overheated gas bottle ruptured, followed by crashes as heat made chunks of melting snow fall down from tree branches.

Robin had taught him basic archery skills, and Matt was a decent shot from close range. His big worry was that one of the bandits would start shooting, but he couldn't spot either gun amid the chaos so he took aim at the three lads who'd been tormenting Robin.

The torso is the easiest target. Matt hit the first teenager in the chest and the other in the shoulder as he turned away. The third guy fell as he tried to escape, but Matt's attempt to shoot him in the arse missed by a few centimetres.

'Don't shoot!' Robin shouted, hands aloft, as he sprinted towards Matt.

Both boys ducked when they heard a gunshot, but when Matt looked around it was Lyla holding the gun. Ten Man took a bandit out with a single punch, then effortlessly picked two off the ground and bashed their heads together.

Robin had a muddy face and felt tearful as he looked at Matt, but he still managed a joke. 'Who said you could use my bow?'

Matt smiled back. 'Someone had to save your sorry arse.'

Lyla fired a warning shot into the air, and the bandits scattered.

'Clear your stuff,' Ten Man shouted. 'Don't let me see any of you within fifty kilometres of here!'

'Not bad for Marion's annoying little brother,' Robin told Matt, giving him a big slap on the back. 'What blew up?'

'The old gas-bottle trick,' Matt explained.

Matt soaked up Robin's praise and cracked a huge smile. But reality kicked in when the youngster looked around the remains of the camp.

The scruffy little girl who'd surprised Robin on the debris mound was there, looking lost and screaming. The dog whimpered, the pregnant woman was having a panic attack, and one of the sadistic teens was bleeding from a huge chest wound, with no chance of getting to a hospital.

Matt had done what was needed to rescue his friends, but the result didn't feel like something he should be proud of.

'Are we all healthy?' Ten Man asked, closing in on the boys, Lyla a few steps behind.

'I've had better mornings,' Lyla moaned. Matt and Robin nodded wearily. 'Let's get our gear and march the hell out of here.'

# 7. CHILLY DIGS

Before the rebels took control of the luxurious Sherwood Castle Resort, the twelfth-floor penthouse had been home to Sheriff Marjorie Kovacevic and her son Little John. Robin had called dibs on the apartment when the rebels arrived and he now shared it with the sprawling Maid family, which included his best friend Marion, her mums Indio and Karma, plus her four annoying little brothers.

But while marble floors, designer furniture and even part of Sheriff Marjorie's art collection remained, day-to-day living was stressful because the castle's electricity supply had been cut. This meant no heating and no elevators. The solar batteries the rebels had set up only gave enough juice for basic lighting and low-voltage appliances, and the limited hot water went to communal showers in the resort's ground-floor swimming pool.

It was just after 1pm. Marion's little brother Otto was brum-brumming toy cars along the marble hallway as Robin stepped in, breathless after climbing twenty-six flights of stairs. Karma heard him arrive and came out of the kitchen holding her baby, Zack.

'We heard Ten Man's radio message when you approached the castle perimeter,' Karma told Robin sympathetically. 'Sounds like you had a rough morning.'

'We needed the money in that safe *so* badly,' Robin said bitterly, catching his breath and walking into the fancy kitchen to refill his water canteen. 'Dr Gladys has Forest People turning up at the clinic with frostbite every day and she's not even got basic stuff, like sterile bandages and antibiotics.'

'Don't blame yourself,' Karma said resolutely. 'Is Matt OK?'

'He'll live,' Robin said. 'The gas explosion caught his forehead and the back of one hand where he shielded his eyes. But it's more like sunburn than serious damage.'

'Indio's on her way down to meet Matt at the medical unit,' Karma said.

Robin guzzled some water before answering. 'I passed her on the stairs. Is Marion around?'

'She had a bite of lunch and headed down to school.'

'I've got mud in my hair and down my back, so I have to shower,' Robin said. 'But there's loads of people queuing for showers, so I'll stand in my bath and wash with cold.'

Karma made Robin a sandwich while he stood in the plush marble shower of the luxurious, but unheated, bedroom he shared with Marion and Matt. Robin's technique for a cold shower was to strip quickly, wet a bar of soap and lather up all over, then he took a deep breath and turned on the icy water to scrub and rinse in a mad twenty-second frenzy.

'So cold!' Robin howled to himself, shuddering as he towelled off at warp speed. Then he dressed in two T-shirts, a hoodie, thick tracksuit bottoms, one pair of normal socks and one pair of long Macondo United football socks that he could tuck his trackie bottoms into.

'You can go down to School Zone when you've eaten,' Karma said, giving Robin a sausage sandwich and a mug of hot chocolate with floating marshmallows.

Robin shook his head. 'I was up at half five, I've walked over twenty kilometres, I've been kicked and slapped. Afternoon lessons have already started, so it's hardly worth it.'

'One and a half lessons won't kill you,' Karma said. 'We agreed that you and Marion could miss school sometimes to help the rebel cause, but—'

Robin finished Karma's sentence in a groany singsong voice, 'But our education is *terribly* important.'

Robin realised he could have exaggerated one of his minor injuries, or just said he had a really bad headache to get out of afternoon school, but Karma would see through the ruse if he tried it on now. So he grabbed his school pack and walked down twenty flights to a row of third-floor conference rooms that were being used to educate one hundred and ninety school-age kids who either lived in the castle or came in from homes in the forest.

The space was fitted out for business meetings, but corporate blandness had been replaced with finger paintings, macaroni pictures and a science project on epigenetics.

The best thing about School Zone was that it was one of the few areas deemed worthy of being heated with the castle's meagre supply of solar electricity. After the frosty hike and a cold shower, Robin loved the waft of heat as he opened the door of the admin office where you had to report if you were late.

The worst thing about School Zone was that it was run by Mr Khan, a strict ex-cop who didn't approve of kids taking time out of lessons to steal trucks or find safes. Khan wasn't around, but Robin was surprised to see his best friend Marion at a little desk at the side of the room. She wore a mad purple wig and was doing some kind of worksheet.

'Hair suits you,' Robin said, smiling at his friend as he warmed his hands over a radiator.

Marion pointed at Mr Khan's desk. 'Our beloved leader has made yet another new rule,' she explained. 'Khan says there's too much disturbance with kids arriving at random times. If you're late now, you have to work here in isolation for the rest of the day.'

'He makes so many rules, I'm amazed he remembers them himself,' Robin said, then his gaze was drawn up towards a vague thud-thud-thud sound.

'I heard the safe was empty,' Marion said. 'After all the work we put into robbing that cash machine . . .'

'Life's depressing right now,' Robin moaned. 'Cold all the time, no money, Khan running this school like military boot camp.'

'Speaking of hair, what happened to yours?' Marion asked.

Robin felt around the back of his head, where his tormentor had chopped the lump out, but he didn't answer because the thudding was getting loud.

'Sound like a chopper to you?' Marion asked anxiously. The last time she'd heard helicopters, they'd dropped firebombs and destroyed her home.

'Might see it through the big windows down the end of the hallway,' Robin suggested.

Marion looked down at her worksheet. 'I'd better not. Khan's already got it in for me.'

Robin gave a superior smile. 'Khan hasn't clocked me yet, so I'm outta here.'

He backed out to a carpeted hallway and headed for a self-service café with a huge bay window at the end. It was definitely a helicopter. By the time he'd got close to the glass and looked up, Marion had changed her mind and stepped up beside him.

'Khan moans about everything,' she explained. 'I may as well give him something worth moaning about.'

Robin saw an aged neon-orange rescue helicopter skimming low around the castle's furthest turret. Nothing had landed at the castle in months, but the pilot was going for the maintenance area behind the castle, because deep snow covered the helipad up on the tenth floor.

'I'm gonna head back and be nosy,' Robin said. 'You coming?'

# 8. THE MAN FROM TWOTU

Robin and Marion didn't want adults asking why they were out of school, so they used the bare concrete emergency stairs to get down to the first floor, then a long service corridor, built so that staff could use it to move room service trolleys and messy cleaners' carts without disturbing Sherwood Castle Resort's ultra-posh guests in the public corridors.

After passing flood-damaged aluminium cabinets and huge gas stoves in the resort's main kitchen, the pair stepped outside into a little alcove with a low wall, designed to keep bins filled with kitchen waste out of sight.

As Marion and Robin crouched at the end of the wall and tucked their hands under their armpits to keep warm, the battered rescue helicopter touched down, making a blizzard out of the fresh snow. It was clearly a friendly visit, because rebel leader Will Scarlock and his wife Emma walked briskly towards the landing site as the blades slowed down.

'Never seen Will in a smart jacket before,' Robin noted.

'Someone important . . .' Marion mused.

A co-pilot jumped out. The copter's air of dilapidation was enhanced as he removed a bungee hook that was keeping the sliding passenger door shut.

'You wouldn't get me up in that box of bolts,' Marion said.

Robin saw a couple of other people watching the mysterious landing from the windows of guest rooms on the floors above. The first passenger to step out of the helicopter was a wild-looking woman in her twenties. She had purple streaks in dark hair, striped leggings, wellies with pictures of superheroes on, and pierced everything.

'Is she famous?' Robin asked Marion quietly. 'I can never remember names, but I know that face from somewhere . . .'

'Not that I know of,' Marion said, then gawped as she recognised the squat, dark-skinned man who came out behind her. He wore a large baseball cap with the bill down over his face, like he didn't want to be recognised.

'That's Rex Lairde,' Marion said disbelievingly. 'Right?'

'Can't be . . .' Robin answered, watching the man shake Will and Emma's hands. 'But it *really* looks like him.'

Rex Lairde was ranked as the richest man in Africa, and fifth wealthiest in the world, founder and Chief Executive Officer of TwoTu Inc., and owner of three major sports teams and the world's biggest superyacht.

'He must be pissed off that we're stealing his vans,' Marion said warily.

Robin laughed, louder than he should when they were supposed to be hiding. 'Yeah, Marion.' He snorted. 'Rex Lairde is worth eighty gazillion dollars, but he's hunting you down personally because you nicked one delivery van.'

Robin's snarky tone annoyed Marion. 'OK, smartass, why *is* he here?' she growled.

Robin kept laughing, so Marion flicked his ear. Meanwhile, Rex Lairde's bodyguard was last out of the helicopter. Dressed in a black catsuit and a full head taller than her boss, she'd have passed for a fashion model if she held a designer handbag instead of a gold-plated Uzi machine gun.

The bodyguard glanced around suspiciously as Will Scarlock led his guests away from the helicopter, up four steps and through the sliding patio doors of Tortilla Durango, a Mexican grill and bar that had been one of Sherwood Castle Resort's casual dining options.

'Gotta see what they're up to,' Marion said keenly, leading the way back inside.

The grill had its own kitchen, but supplies and room service orders went out through a back corridor connected to the main kitchen, so Robin and Marion only had a short walk to get there. They peered into the cantina through the little windows in a set of swing doors.

Like most of Sherwood Castle Resort's ground floor, Tortilla Durango had suffered severe flood damage before the rebels took over. The bar was smashed up, mildewed chairs and broken tables were mounded near the patio entrance, and a stain a metre and a half up the walls marked the high point of the floodwater.

But an area in the centre of the restaurant had been cleared for the meeting, with a table and chairs brought down from an upper floor. Emma Scarlock joined Rex Lairde and the woman in superhero wellies at the table, while the bodyguard kept a wary eye from the entrance and Will said something as he filled glasses with water from an iced decanter.

'Can't hear a word,' Marion told Robin, as she watched Lairde's steamy breath rise into the chilly air.

Robin eyed the dirty, toppled room service trolleys around the base of the staircase that staff had once used to bring food to guests on the restaurant's upstairs balcony.

'We might hear from up there,' he suggested.

'Or we might get shot by Rex Lairde's guard,' Marion said. But she still followed Robin as he ran between the metal trolley legs and up the stairs.

# 9. IT'S THE DOGS

'I thought someone was pulling my leg when you contacted me,' Will Scarlock told Rex Lairde as he settled at the table, along with wife Emma and the woman with the piercings.

The power in Tortilla Durango was off, so Robin and Marion crawled across the shadowy upper floor. They were wary of being seen through the balcony railings, but settled under a table close enough to hear the adults' conversation.

Rex Lairde laughed at Will's comment. Then he started to speak. He had a South African accent and the authority of someone used to being in charge. 'Big bloody problem, Will! Every time I pick up the telephone and say I'm Rex Lairde, people assume I'm making prank calls. They even tell me that the impression I'm doing is no good.'

Will and Emma laughed politely before Lairde continued.

'TwoTu suffered a monstrous ransomware attack two months back. Hackers locked us out of critical data systems in six of our warehouses, and threatened to take down the entire TwoTu website if we didn't pay a ransom of $200 million.'

Emma looked surprised. 'I don't remember hearing about that.'

'We managed to keep the situation under our hats. We lost some deliveries, several warehouses shut down, but the ransomware attack never became public.'

'Did the hackers get their $200 million?' Will asked bluntly.

'We strung them along,' Lairde explained. 'Buying time. Offering ten million, then twenty. All while my IT team figured out a workaround for the hack, and this young lady worked 24/7 to track them down.'

Lairde pointed at the woman with the piercings sitting next to him, then explained who she was.

'D'Angela here heads up special investigations for TwoTu's cybersecurity team. She was extremely successful in tracking down the hackers who held us to ransom. Five people were arrested and face prison time when their case comes to trial. D'Angela's work also kept TwoTu's reputation for reliability and data security intact, and helped police to track down over £70 million that the gang had forced people and businesses to pay in previous ransomware attacks.'

Robin was fascinated by anything to do with hacking. He crawled forward to get a better look at

D'Angela, but backed off when she seemed to glance his way.

'How does your visit here connect with this ransomware attack?' Emma Scarlock asked.

'The hackers who were arrested were under the protection of a powerful Russian mafia group,' Lairde said. 'They did not take kindly to having TwoTu take down their best hacking team – and costing them $70 million. And since they no longer fancied their chances going up against TwoTu in the virtual world, they decided to get physical. Ten days ago, a bunch of goons smashed into my Capital City penthouse and took my precious babies.'

Will and Emma expected to see a girlfriend or child when Lairde unlocked his phone to show a picture. But they saw a professionally lit shot of four large dogs against a white background. They had cream-coloured coats and unusual dreadlocked fur that made them look like giant shaggy floor mops.

'Komondors,' Lairde explained. 'Otherwise known as Hungarian Sheepdogs, or, less flatteringly, mop dogs.'

'They're unusual,' Emma noted. 'Quite beautiful too.'

Lairde smiled at the compliment. 'Their financial value is only a few thousand pounds, but my family has been breeding this line of dogs since I was a boy. To me they're priceless.'

'How much do they want you to pay to get the dogs back?' Will asked, noticing D'Angela distractedly tapping away at her phone.

'They want one hundred million,' Lairde said. 'Seventy to compensate for the money the police seized and thirty to compensate for the loss of the hackers. They've given me two weeks to organise the payment, after which the kidnappers say they will shoot one dog every five days until I do.'

'But we can't trust that group,' D'Angela added, still looking at her phone. 'Even if Mr Lairde pays, they might ask for more.'

Rex Lairde nodded and narrowed his eyes. 'I could not have made TwoTu a success without a reputation for strength. I love my dogs, but I will *not* pay a cent to those dirtbags. If I show weakness by paying out a large ransom, every crook in South Africa, Russia and the rest of the bloody world will start looking for ways to rip me off.'

'I still don't get where we fit in to this,' Will said.

Before Will got his answer, a deafening klaxon erupted. Robin gasped as he took his vibrating phone from his pocket.

'Put it on silent, doofus,' Marion said, then frantically tried to crawl out of sight, hitting her head on the underside of a dining table as she went.

Robin glanced at his phone. Pixelated zombies ran all over his screen, banging up against the sides and saying, 'Let me out' in speech bubbles. When he pressed the volume or tried to unlock it, the buttons were dead.

'I don't know what it's doing,' Robin told Marion, exasperated, trying to scramble away behind her.

Down below, Lairde's bodyguard dropped into a shooting stance but D'Angela stood and made a *don't bother* gesture.

'Stop sneaking around and come join us, Robin Hood,' D'Angela yelled. 'Mr Lairde won't mind, and if you're lucky I'll explain how *pathetically* easy it was to hack your phone.'

# 10. SOMEWHAT EMBARRASSING

Robin was still locked out of his zombie-infested phone as he walked down the curved wooden staircase towards Tortilla Durango's first floor, a sheepish Marion a few steps behind. Will and Emma Scarlock looked furious, but Rex Lairde smirked and D'Angela strode across to meet them.

'If you tap the top of the screen four times you'll get back control of your phone,' D'Angela told Robin as she got close. 'But you have to stop downloading random games and apps every time you're bored, unless you want any halfwit hacker to be able to see all your secrets.'

'You saw me up there and hacked my phone in, like, a minute,' Robin said, impressed but also embarrassed.

As Robin followed D'Angela's instructions and silenced his phone, she held out her hand to him. It had lots of rings and chewed nails.

'D'Angela Dominguez Doncastro,' she announced rapidly, as Robin shook her hand. 'I'm actually a *massive* admirer of yours, Robin. Lots of people in the hacker community say you're a skid. But I say better a skid with the balls to take down bad guys than some brainiac who knows it all but never leaves his mom's basement.'

Robin's wounded expression made Marion curious. 'What's a skid?' she asked.

'Abbreviation of Script Kiddie,' D'Angela explained, with an accent Marion couldn't pin down, still speaking super fast. 'A skid is the lowest rung in the hacker community – when all you can do is hack by uploading other people's scripts, rather than having the programming skills to develop new exploits yourself.'

'I'm only thirteen,' Robin said.

'Just a skid!' Marion said, relishing a new way to tease her best friend.

D'Angela gave a deep laugh. 'I said I was a fan, Robin. Don't sweat it.'

'Why aren't you two in lessons?' Will asked, hands on hips.

Before Robin had to answer, Rex Lairde stepped up and offered Robin his hand to shake.

'The famous outlaw Robin Hood!' he said, cracking a big smile. 'Amazing to meet you!'

Robin wondered if he'd nodded off in class and was about to wake up as his hand got squashed by one of the richest people in the world: a man with plans to build his own space station and who'd allegedly overthrown the South African government when it had tried to make TwoTu pay more tax.

'The famously rich Rex Lairde,' Robin answered cheekily, which made Lairde break into a booming laugh.

Emma grabbed a table and two chairs from a mound the flood had swept them into, then barked at Robin and Marion. 'You two sit there and keep quiet. You should be in school and we'll discuss this later.'

D'Angela wagged her finger and silently mouthed, *you're in trouble*, which made Robin smirk.

'Sit still and zip it!' Emma growled. Will, D'Angela and Lairde settled back at the grown-ups' table.

'So, they kidnapped your dogs,' Will said, picking up Lairde's story. 'You want to get them back without paying the ransom. Since you're here, my guess is that you think they're being held in Sherwood Forest.'

D'Angela nodded. 'I've been able to track the dog-nappers to the forest, but after that the trail goes cold.'

'Probably off-grid,' Robin said from the side table.

Emma gave Robin another look, but D'Angela beamed at him. 'Robin is correct. The bad guys know that Mr Lairde has access to advanced technology and a highly skilled information security unit. The logical thing to do was hide deep in Sherwood Forest.'

'Police and Forest Rangers have no presence in the forest away from major roads,' Lairde said. 'And corruption is so rampant, they're more likely to sell the story of my kidnapped dogs to the media than they are to find them.

'I've got search drones, satellite imagery and all the best tech. But we don't know the forest the way you people do and if we find my dogs, I'll need people who know the forest to stage a rescue operation.'

Will rubbed his palms together awkwardly. 'I'd happily put you in touch with people who can help. But I am in a delicate position. There are hundreds of gangs in Sherwood Forest. My organisation helps Forest People who need food, shelter and medical care, but we're *not* a police force. If rebel security patrols encounter something unjust, we'll do our best to stop it. But if I start sending patrols into the forest to hunt people down, I'll make a lot of enemies.'

'More enemies than we have the resources to fight,' Emma added.

Rex Lairde steepled his fingers and laughed. 'Mr and Mrs Scarlock, it may have escaped your attention, but I am *staggeringly* rich. So here is what I am proposing. First, TwoTu has a medical equipment subsidiary. I understand that you lost all medical equipment when your base at Designer Outlets was burned. As an opening gesture, TwoTu is willing to donate a million pounds' worth of medical equipment.'

Will's eyes lit up; Forest People regularly suffered or died due to poor medical care. But on the other hand . . .

'Most modern medical gear is of little use without electricity,' Emma said. 'For example, Dr Gladys would love an X-ray machine. But they use twenty kilowatts, which is more than we have to power the entire castle on a cloudy day.'

Lairde nodded. 'Which brings me to the second part of my offer. TwoTu has been investing heavily in renewable energy for our warehouses and state-of-the-art electric delivery vehicles.'

Robin and Marion gawped. Will and Emma looked wary.

'Have you really?' Will said, trying to look innocent.

'We recently opened a vehicle charging station on Route 24, less than four kilometres from here. My chief electrical engineer says she can restore power to Sherwood Castle by laying an eight-hundred-metre high-voltage cable between the TwoTu charging station and the existing power lines that fed Sherwood Castle before Sheriff Marjorie had your electricity cut off.

'You'll have all the power you need for as long as you need it. In return, I want you to give D'Angela a quiet space to work here at Sherwood Castle. When she locates the scum who stole my dogs, I want you to make your *best* people available to help with a rescue mission.'

'We'd have to be discreet,' Will said, after a pause. 'Sheriff Marjorie's people will start sniffing around if Sherwood Castle suddenly lights up at night.'

'Discretion is in all of our interests,' Rex Lairde agreed. 'I don't want word to get out that I'm setting up an illegal electricity connection between a TwoTu charging station and the base of a banned terrorist group. And I'm sure you don't want the world to know that you've cut a deal with one of those evil profit-obsessed billionaires that folks like you are supposed to despise.'

Will wasn't comfortable with Lairde's proposal, but felt that he was someone they could do business with.

'Power and medical equipment will save lives,' Emma told her husband keenly. Then to Lairde, 'The electricity stays on for as long as we need it?'

Lairde nodded. 'But if the illegal connection is unearthed by Forest Rangers or the Sheriff's people, I will have to deny all knowledge and say it was installed by rebels without anyone from TwoTu knowing.'

'Sounds fair,' Will said.

Lairde reached across the table to shake on the deal. 'One last thing before I head home,' he said, withdrawing his outstretched hand.

'What?' Will asked.

Lairde cracked a big smile. 'You have to stop stealing my bloody delivery vans.'

Marion and Robin laughed as the rebel leader and the tax-dodging billionaire shook hands.

# 11. OUT OF KHAN'S GRASP

Eight centimetres of snow had fallen overnight. As Robin stepped out of his room into the penthouse's marble hallway, Marion's little brothers Finn and Otto were crashing around on the balcony having a snowball fight.

'Morning, all,' Robin said, rubbing his hands to stay warm as he walked into the kitchen for breakfast. 'Is it me, or is today even colder?'

Karma was changing baby Zack's nappy near the door. Robin tried not to inhale as he passed by. Matt and Marion were already stuffing their faces with breakfast at the long marble-topped dining table. Since the swanky kitchen's six-ring induction hob had no power, Indio was using a two-ring gas camping stove to cook scrambled eggs and keep a saucepan of milk warm.

'Forecast said it's minus nine,' Matt said as Robin put Cheerios in a bowl, then held it out for Indio to pour on hot milk.

'Eggs won't be long, and there's heaps of bread,' Indio said.

Karma put Zack in his high chair then yelled for the two squealing boys on the balcony to come inside for breakfast, then yelled at them again to take their shoes off before they traipsed water all over the marble floors.

'You two are soaked,' Indio complained when Finn and Otto stumbled in, red-cheeked and breathless. 'You've only just got over colds and coughs.'

Otto cracked a huge fart as he lined up for his hot milk. Marion looked furious.

'Can I get through one meal without having to inhale microscopic particles of someone else's poop?' she complained.

Robin's laugh was stifled because he was starving, and his cheeks were stuffed with bread dunked in hot milk from his cereal bowl. Maid family meals were always noisy and chaotic, but Robin loved them because they made him feel like he had a proper family, even though his mum was dead and his dad was in prison.

'You want eggs?' Matt asked Robin.

'Cheers, mate,' Robin said.

'Me too, while you're up,' Marion said.

'Only got two hands,' Matt told his sister, handing Robin a plate stacked with rich yellow scrambled eggs, then giving Marion the finger.

Marion tried to steal Matt's eggs, but he swept them out of reach.

'So predictable,' Matt taunted.

'Sheila's eggs are the best,' Robin said, tucking in as Finn and Otto settled on his side of the table's long bench seat.

'Did you help in the chicken sheds this morning?' Karma asked Robin as she checked the temperature of Zack's bottle.

'Only twice a week now,' Robin said. 'With food so hard to come by, Sheila's got heaps of volunteers who'll work all day for a tray of eggs. And I might not be able to go at all this week if I'm gonna be helping D'Angela set up her gear.'

Marion tutted. 'I can't believe you got out of school *again*.'

Matt flung himself back from the table excitedly, like he'd had the best idea in history. 'Oh, Robin, yeah! Can you ask D'Angela if she needs another assistant?'

'She wants me because of my hacking skills,' Robin said.

Marion smirked. 'If you say so, *skid*.'

'But I rescued you yesterday,' Matt told Robin. 'You *owe* me. Please just ask?'

'Matt's got a maths test today,' Otto explained. 'He's desperate to get out of it.'

Indio cut in before Robin could answer. 'Matthew Maid, your last grades were terrible,' she began. 'Mr Khan called me down twice in the last month because you've been fighting, and you missed a whole day of school yesterday. So to be clear: your chances of getting another day off school are the same as my chances of sitting down and eating a meal in peace before you lot all grow up and leave home.'

'I didn't make you have so many babies,' Matt blurted furiously.

Robin tried not to laugh as Karma told Matt off for being cheeky. Otto suggested that Matt should be grounded for a month, and Finn knocked his cereal bowl over.

'Thanks for breakfast – gotta go meet D'Angela!' Robin said as he put his cutlery in the sink and bolted for the penthouse exit.

# 12. THE NEST

Robin took his thick winter coat and phone from his room, then charged down twenty-two flights to the ground floor. D'Angela gave Robin a big smile when they met in the resort's flood-damaged reception.

'Sleep OK?' Robin asked.

'Kinda,' D'Angela said. 'Had a boozy dinner with the Scarlock family after Rex Lairde left and Will set me up with a nice hotel room, but this building is creepy at night with nothing but torchlight. It took three duvets to stay warm, and I gave up on showering because the queue was massive.'

'I'd like to tell you you'll get used to it,' Robin said, half smiling. 'But when it's this cold it's basically crap all the time.'

'Will arranged for the hacking and surveillance equipment I need to be carried in through the forest overnight,' D'Angela said. 'Since we want as few people as possible to know what I'm doing here, Will has had it taken to the casino security office up on the third floor. But I'm not sure where that is.'

Around five hundred rebels had made Sherwood Castle their new home, while a transient population of refugees and Forest People who needed shelter meant over a thousand people typically slept under Sherwood Castle's roof each night.

But everyone stuck to the hotel towers and upstairs lobby where there was light – and very occasionally heat. The rest of the vast resort, from wedding chapels and conference venues to the golf course clubhouses and the sprawling Blue Monday nightclub, was utterly deserted.

Robin showed D'Angela the way to her new operations room. They walked over a thick, luxurious carpet past the second-floor casino's roulette wheels and slot machines.

'So where are you from originally?' Robin asked as they walked.

'Can't you tell from my accent?' D'Angela teased, then after a pause said, 'Argentina.'

Robin tried to think of something he knew about Argentina, but only came up with, 'That's South America, right?'

'Right,' D'Angela said, mocking Robin's tone.

'Is hacking big there?' Robin asked.

'Hell, yes,' D'Angela said enthusiastically. 'You ever hear of Ekoparty? That's where I first made my name in the community.'

'Is it like a club or something?'

'It's the biggest infosec gathering outside of the United States,' D'Angela explained. 'Thousands of hackers, spies and industry people come to Buenos Aires for three whole days. Most are just skids and wannabes, some as young as you.'

'Many girls?' Robin queried.

'Not many,' D'Angela said. 'You learn heaps. Famous hackers give talks, there are workshops, parties, steal-the-flag challenges and stuff. But if you want to make a name for yourself, the most important part is hackathons. They set you a hacking challenge and your team gets a few hours to beat it.'

'Sounds awesome,' Robin said. 'Though I wouldn't get far since I'm just a skid who uses other people's work.'

D'Angela laughed. 'Hopefully I'll be around long enough to start turning you into a real hacker . . . So, my first Ekoparty, I was thirteen and my dad said I couldn't go. But I skipped school, bought a ticket and rode the bus for six hours. My parents had this little computer repair shop/internet café type thing, way out in cattle country.'

Robin grinned. 'My dad taught computer repairs.'

'I read your story in the news.' D'Angela smiled back. 'That's one of the many reasons I'm a fan of your work.'

Robin was glad the casino was dark, because his cheeks flushed.

'I arrived at Ekoparty with two older guys from my town who were also into hacking. It's sketchy now I look back on it, because we barely had money for food, let alone a safe place to sleep. We entered one of the big hackathons and placed fifth, which doesn't sound amazing, but we were schoolkids and all the teams ahead of us were security industry professionals or university graduates.

'We spent our first night sleeping at the bus station scared of getting robbed. Second night we were at some fancy cocktail party run by a big Chinese tech company. People were giving us business cards and offering hotel rooms and dinners, telling us how they want to work with us or give us money to study.'

'That's cool,' Robin said. 'But why did you get so much attention?'

'People with top hacking skills are always in demand,' D'Angela explained. 'All the big cybersecurity and technology companies attend every major hacking conference in the world, looking for recruits. And intelligence agencies are there too – China, Russia, USA. All the big European countries send agents. They're usually disguised as businesspeople, but everyone knows who they really are.'

Robin had reached a curtained wall at the far end of the casino. He pulled back a curtain to reveal a hidden door.

'What did your parents do when you got home?' he asked as he went through the unlocked door and up a precariously dark staircase.

'My mum gave me the lashing of a lifetime,' D'Angela said. 'But the name of our crew was out in the hacker community. We got a story in the local newspaper. We got invited to visit the US to tour a couple of big tech companies' headquarters. We entered more hackathons and had universities offering us scholarships. Not many poor Argentinian girls get to study for free in Berkeley and Beijing.'

'Or end up working as Rex Lairde's chief hacker,' Robin pointed out.

As Robin rounded the top of the stairs, he saw sunshine coming through a pair of skylights. He stepped into a large control room known as the Nest. The screens along one wall were linked to cameras overlooking the empty casino below, built to watch gamblers and dealers and ensure nobody stole or cheated.

Out of habit, D'Angela flipped the light switch. Nothing happened.

'We're working in the gloom until your boss gets the electric on,' Robin joked. Then his attention switched to the mountain of new IT equipment that had been brought up by the team that carried it through the forest. 'Have you got enough stuff here?'

Robin looked awed as he circled boxes containing satellite dishes, a solar battery, drones and listening devices, along with more ordinary stuff like computer mice and screens.

'When your boss is a billionaire in a hurry, you get anything you ask for,' D'Angela said. 'I hear your climbing skills are pretty good, so you can start by helping me fit satellite dishes on the roof.'

'Anything's better than school,' Robin agreed, eyeing a stack of laptops. 'I had this amazing gaming laptop, but the Sheriff's people hacked me and blew it up.'

'Battery overrun hack?' D'Angela asked.

'Yeah,' Robin admitted weakly.

'Amateurish,' D'Angela said harshly, shaking her head.

'Cost me over two thousand, *and* I lost all my savings in the fire at Designer Outlets. Now if I want to use a laptop, I have to beg Marion or Indio.'

'A hacker without a computer.' D'Angela laughed, making sad eyes and playing an imaginary violin. 'I guess climbing on an icy roof fixing up a satellite internet connection qualifies you for danger money. So, take one of those laptops. But you're not gonna switch it on until I've shown you how to *properly* secure a new laptop – and fix that security-nightmare phone you're carrying around.'

# 13. ELITE-LEVEL SURVEILLANCE

Robin spent two days in and around the Nest with D'Angela, and loved every minute. They killed their arms and shoulders shovelling snow from the flat roof above the casino, then set up solar panels, satellite dishes and several antennae. Inside they rigged three regular computers and a supercomputer built for artificial intelligence.

The Super, as D'Angela called it, came in a bright green TwoTu-branded cabinet roughly the size of a dishwasher. It contained dozens of processors and high-end graphics cards and ran EyeZ data lake software developed by the United States Secret Service. It could sort and find patterns in billions of pieces of data, using a mixture of raw computing power and artificial intelligence.

Robin was awed when the system started up, using the large rooftop aerials to sniff out local phone signals, Wi-Fi traffic and the two-way radios popular among the better equipped forest groups. Additional data streams like live weather and hacked data from 5G phone masts were downloaded via a satellite internet connection.

The EyeZ software brought all the data streams together into a data lake, then overlaid the results on a zoomable map of Sherwood Forest. Seconds after going live the giant main screen showed hundreds of dots as the system pinpointed the locations of phones, satellite uplinks, Wi-Fi networks and even the live position of Forest Ranger drones.

Another important stream in the data lake was thermal mapping provided by satellite. When D'Angela connected this data to the map they could zoom in close and detect heat signatures from fires, solar panels and even a herd of deer crossing open ground.

As well as showing where the thousands of communication signals came from, EyeZ could record and analyse them. Messages that used advanced encryption couldn't be read, but were a sign that people might have something to hide. Anything sent unencrypted or with weak encryption was decoded, then checked against a list of keywords.

So, if anyone in the forest sent a message containing words related to dogs, kidnapping, ransoms, Rex Lairde, or more than a hundred other trigger words D'Angela had chosen, the Super showed it as a green triangle on the map and added it to a list of messages for D'Angela to read.

An hour after being switched on, the combination of radio signals, online data and EyeZ surveillance software had built a map of Sherwood showing the probable location of more than a thousand camps and settlements, a rough guide to how many people lived in each one and, in many cases, enough decoded messages to know what they were up to.

'I'm guessing the dog-nappers won't risk staying in a large settlement,' D'Angela explained to Robin, as he zoomed around the on-screen map in a state of fascination. 'They'll try to stay off-grid, but they'll still need to communicate regularly. My best guess is that we're looking for a settlement with less than ten people. If they're trying to stay off-grid, signals will pop up around the settlement rather than inside it.'

Robin furrowed his brow and spoke thoughtfully. 'It's hard to get a mobile signal in most parts of the forest, and not many settlements have their own satellite connections. You'll probably find loads of groups who move away from their camp when they need to communicate.'

'Hadn't thought of that,' D'Angela admitted cheerfully. 'This is why having you here is useful.'

But her positive mood didn't last, because the lights in the Nest blacked out. Screens, apart from one battery-powered laptop, died and the Super's big cooling fans whirred to a stop.

'What's wrong now?' D'Angela moaned, switching on her phone to make some light.

Robin grabbed a torch and crawled around the equipment, hoping to find a tripped fuse or a loose wire. Then D'Angela hit the test button on their giant lithium battery pack.

'Dead flat,' she announced.

Robin was on his knees at the back of the Super. His cheek was blasted by heat when he got too close – its metal case was too hot to touch.

'Heat means energy, right?' Robin said as his torch beam picked out D'Angela a few metres across the floor. 'The Super was nowhere near this hot before all the data streams got plugged in.'

D'Angela clearly saw what Robin was thinking.

'How did I miss that?' she said, shaking her head furiously. 'I calculated that two solar batteries and twenty square metres of panels would be enough to keep the Super running 24/7. But the power drain is way higher when it's analysing all that data.'

Robin looked up through one of the skylights at the winter evening sky, which had a hint of moonlight. 'Solar won't give us any more juice until sunrise.'

'I'll get more panels and batteries brought in through the forest overnight,' D'Angela said, already tapping an email on her phone to sort it out.

'We won't need solar if your boss gets mains power hooked up,' Robin pointed out. 'You got any more info on that?'

'It's coming,' D'Angela answered, eyes fixed on her phone. 'But it's taking longer than we expected.'

Robin admired D'Angela, but he didn't entirely trust her. Rex Lairde hadn't become one of the richest people in the world by being a nice guy, and Robin wondered if the tantalising promise of mains electricity would get dangled like a carrot on a stick until the billionaire got his precious dogs back . . .

# 14. THE EGG LADY

'If there's no power, we're done for today,' D'Angela told Robin, brushing dust off her jeans as she got up from the floor of the Nest. 'I'll get some food with the Scarlocks, try to sleep under my mound of duvets, and we'll make a fresh start tomorrow.'

'Sounds like a plan,' Robin said. 'I told my other boss, Chicken Sheila, that I'd drop by her poultry sheds and check the incubators when I got a chance. She's crazier than a bag of spiders and the ammonia in chicken poop makes your eyes water. But on the plus side, the sheds have oil heating and we've managed to keep the tanks full, so it's toasty if you want to tag along.'

Robin's offer wasn't the most attractive D'Angela had ever received, but she faced hours in her chilly sixth-floor hotel room, or hanging out with the Scarlock clan, who didn't seem comfortable socialising with someone who worked for TwoTu.

'This is my new pal, D'Angela,' Robin told Chicken Sheila after they'd walked to the animal sheds behind the castle.

In the rebels' previous base at Designer Outlets, Sheila kept her birds in two roughly built wooden sheds on the roof. She was building up a new flock at Sherwood Castle with the benefit of a long metal silo that had been designed to hold the exotic animals that had been released into the castle's hunting grounds and shot by wealthy hunters.

Sheila's new flock was far from complete, so her birds had loads of space and a couple of teenaged volunteers strolled among them throwing them handfuls of greenery picked from the castle grounds. But while the birds looked happy, Sheila was pale, and thinner than when Robin had rescued her from the burning mall rooftop a few months earlier.

The old lady sat barking orders at her assistants now, when in the past she'd made a point of working harder than anyone else. There were rumours that Sheila was sick, but when Robin asked, she scowled and told him to mind his own business.

'You're from Argentina,' Sheila said brusquely after D'Angela said hello.

D'Angela was impressed. 'Nobody ever gets my accent.'

'I had a husband from Argentina a million years ago,' Sheila explained. 'Looked sexy in a suit, but he turned out to be a complete knob.'

Robin was surprised. He'd spent hundreds of hours working alongside Sheila but never heard her mention a husband before.

'I suppose you'll be after my biscuits,' Sheila told Robin as he filled a kettle to make tea.

'Gonna scoff the lot,' Robin teased, giving Sheila a cheeky flick with one eyebrow. 'Is that incubator I fixed still working?'

'He's a good boy, really,' Sheila told D'Angela, making Robin feel about five years old. 'Just keep a close eye so he doesn't slack off.'

As Robin let the kettle boil and began to check that the three incubator cabinets where eggs hatched were running at the right temperature, D'Angela peered through a metal archway and saw five larger animals in a gloomy adjoining shed.

'Zebras!' D'Angela gasped, stepping into the archway. 'Why?'

'Truckload of zebras crashed on Route 24 back in the spring,' Robin explained, taking three mugs and a box of teabags from a metal cabinet. 'Quite a few got butchered or drowned during the summer floods. The first two were rescued and brought here when one of our patrols found them suffering from cold. Others got brought in by random people. It's too cold to set them free, and Will's had no luck finding a better home for them.'

'Can I go say hello?' D'Angela asked, smiling childishly.

'Don't get too close,' Sheila warned. 'Zebras look like horses, but a horse won't bite your fingers off.'

'Millions of years getting chased by lions,' Robin said, breathing the earthy smell of manure as he stepped up to the zebra cages behind D'Angela. 'They're basically nutters.'

D'Angela's gaze shifted towards a rack on the far wall, lined with whips, hooks, electric stun sticks and tranquilliser guns.

'Sheriff Marjorie used to pack these sheds with exotic animals, then set them loose in the castle grounds and let rich people hunt them for *fun*,' Robin explained, then smirked as he picked up a vicious-looking stun stick. 'I'd love to give her fifty thousand volts from one of these and see how she likes it . . .'

# 15. MARKET DAY

As well as offering emergency food, shelter and medical care to thousands of Forest People, Will Scarlock's rebels ran a weekly market. It was a social hub for news and gossip, and the only place where Forest People could buy and sell without the risk of being robbed by bandits, or shaken down by gangsters or corrupt cops if they ventured into a town like Locksley without identity papers.

The market at Designer Outlets had been on the rooftop, but at Sherwood Castle Resort it took place inside a huge hall built for trade shows and conferences. Outsiders were searched for weapons on entry, but Robin still had a bounty on his head, so he carried his bow and knew that the security teams who watched the market closely would have eyes on him at all times.

Robin had been working up in the Nest with D'Angela for eight days and the Super had been running for three, with the benefit of more solar power and a diesel back-up generator. Since he was working to rescue a billionaire's dogs, Robin found the nerve to ask for wages and D'Angela had no problem giving away some of Rex Lairde's money.

D'Angela had said she could do without Robin for a couple of hours while he went to the market. After being broke for months, Robin was tempted by a new phone and a stall selling stolen mountain bikes for a fraction of their real cost. But he didn't know when he'd have money in his pocket again, so he stayed practical.

After buying a pair of boots that fitted and a pair to grow into, he bought deodorant, extra gloves, waterproof trousers and packs of socks and underwear. His only non-essential purchases were a book on the history of archery that the man who ran a little book stall had set aside for him, and a wooden sorting block toy that he thought baby Zack would like.

His last stop was a place that did amazing burritos. Robin was asked to sign three photos of himself as he stood in line. It was a fair walk back to the Nest with his and D'Angela's foil-wrapped lunches, so Robin jogged. He didn't notice Marion until she yelled, 'Hey!' after him.

'Hey,' Robin said back, stopping and turning around.

Marion had a new arrival with her. A girl about their age with dried forest mud up her tracksuit bottoms.

'All right for some,' Marion said, as she eyed Robin's shopping bags. 'Getting out of school and making the big bucks.'

'I got this for Zack,' Robin said, tilting the bag with the little sorting toy so Marion could see. 'We didn't save any toys from the fire.'

'Cute,' Marion admitted, as her friend stared shyly at the ground. 'We came for a quick look at the market during school lunch break. Is there any chance D'Angela needs another assistant?'

'Yeah,' Robin scoffed. 'You and your amazing computer skills!'

Marion looked hurt. 'All right, skid,' she growled. 'Guess I'm just the dumb forest kid . . .'

Robin knew Marion was sensitive about growing up in the forest and missing out on education and other stuff that regular kids got. But on the other hand . . .

'You *always* call me a geek and take the mickey when I talk about hacking or computers,' Robin blurted irritably. 'I need to go. I've got hot food for me and D'Angela.'

'Later, potato.' Marion sighed.

Robin was frustrated that he'd upset his best friend, and tried to fix it. 'You want money for burritos?' he asked, peeling a note from a roll of twenties in his pocket.

Marion's friend looked impressed by Robin's supply of cash, but Marion was too proud. She batted Robin's hand away and made kissing noises as he backed off.

'Better run to your girlfriend, D'Angela,' Marion said. 'Tell her hi from me.'

Robin was annoyed as he left the market. Having money and new clothes made him feel good, but now a stupid argument with Marion had trashed his mood.

'How's it going?' Robin asked D'Angela when he got back to the Nest. He put his shopping down and tossed over her burrito.

Extra solar panels and a portable diesel generator meant that the Super could run all day. They'd also rigged up more lights, and moved two desks so they got warmed by the hot blast from the supercomputer's cooling fans.

'That market is a gold mine of information,' D'Angela told Robin. 'EyeZ is analysing speech from the microphone arrays we put on the exhibition centre roof. With everyone using the improved phone mast and resort Wi-Fi we set up, I'm getting *so* much info.'

'Anything exciting while I was gone?' Robin asked, sitting at his desk and biting a chunk out of his burrito.

'There's a stall selling dog food and pet stuff which has got to be worth keeping an eye on,' D'Angela said. Then after a pause, 'Oh my *God*, this burrito! So good!'

'Told you.' Robin smiled. 'I haven't had one for ages because I've been broke, but they're always the best.'

As Robin scoffed more burrito, he nudged the mouse to activate his computer screen.

In quieter moments D'Angela had been giving Robin hacking exercises that needed coding and math skills to solve. But even though Robin was keen to elevate his status from skid to genuine hacker, he closed a window on the computer with D'Angela's latest puzzle and connected to a feed from one of the security cameras that rebel security chief Azeem Masri used to watch over the market.

'Saw this man and woman while I was trying on my new boots,' Robin told D'Angela, skipping back through the CCTV footage. 'I did a hack inside Sherwood Castle six months back—'

'The StayNet system,' D'Angela interrupted, as rice dropped from her burrito and pelted the desk.

'Yeah,' Robin said. 'This couple I saw when I was trying on boots, I could swear I saw both of them working for Sheriff Marjorie, in security.'

'You know how to trace them in EyeZ?' D'Angela asked.

'I remember most of what you taught me,' Robin said, nodding.

Robin found security footage from when he'd been trying on boots. Then he hit play and watched the couple moving around the market, switching to different cameras when they went out of shot. He saw what he wanted when an overhead camera caught the woman taking her phone from a pocket and unlocking it with a fingerprint.

Robin jotted down the exact time that this footage was taken, then opened the EyeZ software and requested a list of devices connected to the local mobile data mast at that moment. A huge list of phone numbers and device IDs scrolled up the screen.

'Am I doing this right?' Robin asked as D'Angela watched from the next desk.

'You've got almost six hundred phones connected,' she explained. 'But if you use the data surge filter, it will tell you which phones requested a big chunk of data. Set the focus slider to two minutes and you'll only see devices that are requesting a large chunk of data for the first time in that time period.'

Robin smiled as the number of listed devices dropped from hundreds to three.

'Now use Autofind?' Robin asked, hovering the mouse over the option box.

'Doesn't always work, but it's great when it does,' D'Angela answered.

When Robin hit Autofind, the EyeZ software took the three phone numbers and began trying to match them against several hundred stolen databases in its data lake. This was the kind of personal data that hackers steal from airlines, online shops, banks and government departments and sell for a few thousand pounds to anyone willing to pay.

'Got her,' Robin said keenly as EyeZ found a scan of the woman's passport that had been emailed to a car insurance company. 'Ruby Cohen-Jones.'

Robin aborted the search on the other two phone numbers and clicked to extend the search on Ruby. Thirty seconds later, EyeZ had checked hundreds of data sources and produced all of Ruby's personal information, several passwords, bank account numbers, her home address and even an online photo album showing Ruby's wedding to the man Robin had seen her with.

'Amazing but creepy,' Robin said. 'I had no idea there was this much stolen data out there.'

D'Angela smiled. 'Dozens of companies and organisations have their customer data hacked every day, and you can buy it all when Rex Lairde tells you to spend whatever it takes.'

Ruby's bank statement confirmed Robin's hunch, showing that her salary used to be paid by Sherwood Forest Resort. More recently, her only income was unemployment benefit, her car was about to be repossessed, and her landlord had filed court papers for unpaid rent on a Locksley apartment.

'I knew I'd seen those two before,' Robin said. 'But why come all the way here from Locksley? I mean, you don't trek through ten kilometres of forest to do your weekly shop. They *must* be up to something.'

D'Angela shrugged. 'I'd bet half the people down in that market are up to something. But we're only paid to care about the ones who kidnapped my boss's dogs.'

'They could be spies working for Sheriff Marjorie or something,' Robin said. 'I should buzz our security chief, Azeem, so she can keep an eye on them.'

D'Angela put the disintegrating remains of her burrito on the desk. She sounded irritated. 'I've got a backlog of eight hundred flagged messages to read. We need to keep watching that pet stall for anyone buying a lot of dog food, and we need to make sure the Super stays cool and doesn't blow another graphics card. But if you've got nothing more productive to do than speculate about two random people, feel free to report back to school.'

Robin looked shocked as he wheeled his chair back from the desk. D'Angela had never snapped at him before, and it made him feel a little sick.

'I . . .' Robin began.

D'Angela changed her tone when she saw she'd hurt Robin's feelings. 'I'm sorry, Robin,' she began, biting her chewed-up thumbnail. 'I've been working fourteen-hour days since the Super went online and I'm barely sleeping in this cold.'

'I know you're stressed,' Robin said. 'It's been snowing, so I'd better go sweep off the solar panels and top up the diesel generator.'

'Good plan,' D'Angela agreed.

As Robin headed up a ladder to the roof, D'Angela freeze-framed some footage from the market, drew a box around a man's face, and clicked a button so that the Super would use facial recognition software to compare his picture against sixty million stolen identity card records.

# 16. HOT BUTTERED TOAST

By half eight that evening, Robin had survived another riotous Maid family dinner and taken refuge in the middle of his enormous bed. He had his head poking out between two thick duvets. Marion and Matt had abandoned their own beds on the floor, snuggling either side of Robin, as the laptop resting across his knees played the latest superhero movie.

Despite the penthouse's marble-clad walls, Robin could still hear chaos as Indio and Karma tried to get seven-year-old Otto, three-year-old Finn and baby Zack to settle for the night.

'Guys!' Otto said breathlessly as he crashed through the bedroom door, wearing pyjamas and fur-lined boots.

'Buzz off, turd-breath!' Matt snapped, whipping a cushion off Robin's bed and flinging it at Otto's head.

'Go to bed,' Marion added stiffly. 'I'm sick of your nonsense every night.'

'Floor's hot in the hallway!' Otto announced cryptically, ducking a second flying cushion and putting his palm against the floor tiles. 'It's the same here.'

'What are you on about?' Robin said, pausing the movie. Marion reached down and touched the tiles.

'He's not wrong,' Marion said, sounding curious. 'It's warm.'

'Mum says it's underfloor heating,' Otto explained.

Robin's spot in the middle meant he was last off the bed, but as he got out he spotted a red pulse from the smoke alarm on the ceiling, which he hadn't seen since the electricity got cut off.

Marion tried a light switch and got nothing, but Karma yelled from the guest bathroom. 'There's warm water from the taps!'

'Electricity!' Marion gasped, hardly daring to believe it, and confused because the light switch hadn't worked.

'They must be switching things on gradually,' Robin guessed. 'Safety checks and stuff.'

Matt and Otto charged into the bathroom as Marion nodded.

'Heat is top priority in this weather,' Marion said. 'And Will said he didn't want the castle all lit up, cos then the Sheriff's people would see we'd got power restored and start asking why.'

'It's so nice,' Otto said, splashing himself with hot water at the bathroom sink.

Robin felt warmth from the underfloor heating through his two pairs of socks as he stepped out into the hallway.

While Sherwood Castle's main lighting circuits hadn't been restored, there was a glow from signs pointing to the emergency exits and when he looked out of the main door into the entrance lobby the lift indicator was lit up, though the screen read *out of order*.

'This is huge!' Robin said cheerfully, walking down to the kitchen where Karma was cuddling baby Zack to sleep.

Back in Robin's bathroom, Matt and Otto battled for control of a shower head, and Marion looked like she'd peed herself after she tried to stop them and came off worst.

'It's running everywhere,' Marion shouted. 'My mattress is right outside this door, and if that gets soggy you two are dead!'

Indio charged into Robin's bedroom, shouting at everyone to stop splashing and behave, and Robin heard a bunch of clicks in the kitchen. Zack turned his little head, startled by the blue *00:00* that had begun to flash on the oven and microwave.

Robin grinned as he opened the microwave and a light came on. Three-year-old Finn was the only member of the Maid family who'd gone to sleep, but now he was up too, looking sleepy and confused as two soggy big brothers hurtled past into the kitchen.

'We can make toast!' Matt shouted, snatching bread off the kitchen table. 'All the plugs are on.'

Otto had beaten Matt to the toaster. 'It was my idea! I'm putting the bread in.'

'You're both dripping!' Karma shouted, loud enough to startle Zack. 'You'll get electrocuted.'

'Stand back, I'll show you,' Robin said, smiling.

Robin smiled as he took charge of the toaster. He'd lived the first twelve years of his life in a regular house, but Matt and Otto were forest kids. The most electricity they'd known was a low-voltage supply for fridges, phone chargers and small lamps, not stuff that needed lots of power like washing machines and toasters.

'I've used the toaster at Aunt Lucy's place,' Matt told Robin indignantly as he dropped the bread in. 'I know what I'm doing.'

Matt and Otto were fascinated as the toaster elements started to glow red, while Finn kept opening and closing the fridge door to make the light come on.

'Dry that floor before someone slips and cracks their head open,' Indio ordered, as she threw Matt and Otto a big towel.

'We'll have to get powder for the washing machine,' Karma told Indio happily. 'No more handwashing underwear in cold water.'

'And fabric softener,' Marion said happily, as Robin started buttering the toast. 'And the boys can have a hot shower *every* day, so I won't have to breathe Matt's foot cheese and Robin's armpits all night . . .'

'I smell fantastic,' Robin protested as he bit into one slice of hot toast and handed the other one to Otto.

'Where's mine?' Matt said before dropping more toast in. '*Both* these slices are for me!'

Before the second round of toast popped up, floor-rumbling electronic dance music started wafting from below. Karma got a text and read it aloud.

> **Nefili and Tasos invite you to celebrate the restoration of power in the eleventh-floor banqueting rooms. We found disco lights and beer is cooling in the fridge!**

'That's my friend Jason's mum and dad!' Otto said cheerfully, then, with pleading eyes, 'Can we go? Can we go?'

Robin had left his phone by his bed, but Marion showed him several texts on her notification screen. All from kids they knew, saying everyone was heading to the eleventh floor to celebrate electricity.

'Social event of the season,' Marion said. 'We have to go!'

'We'll never sleep with all that noise downstairs,' Robin pointed out. 'I'll wear my new boots.'

Indio and Karma looked at each other and smiled. 'All right, you lot, let's celebrate,' Indio said. 'Tomorrow's Saturday, so you don't have to get up for school.'

# 17. WHATSERNAME

Robin woke just before nine on Saturday. He was lying with his boots hanging off a bright red sofa in an eleventh-floor conference room. His neck and back were sweaty, which was a treat after waking up shivering every day for two months.

He remembered jumping around and dancing in disco lights with that lack of self-consciousness you get when everyone else is doing the same. He'd snatched and drunk one beer, but got a stern *don't you dare* from Karma when he tried to grab another. He'd spent ages having an amazing conversation with the refugee girl who'd been with Marion the previous lunchtime and they'd . . .

*We kissed.*

*My first kiss . . .*

The memory gave Robin a bigger smile, because it had been unexpected and cool and maybe he even had a girlfriend now . . .

*But what was her name?*

As Robin sat up, he saw heaps of empty beer bottles all over a table, then puke on the carpet. He dry-heaved.

'Nasty!' Robin groaned, holding his breath as he stumbled out of the room.

The eleventh floor's main hallway was a post-party nightmare of bodies, bottles and abandoned winter clothing. A bunch of wasted older teens caught some fresh air on a balcony, obviously hoping that the cold and cigarettes would take a bite out of their hangovers.

'Robin Hood!' one who looked particularly wasted shouted. 'Come out here, man! We've got hot coffee.'

'Thanks, but I have to take a leak,' Robin answered. He remembered the state of the toilets the night before when all the adults had been drunk, so he headed up to the twelfth-floor penthouse and moved stealthily across the broad marble hallway to the guest bathroom.

Robin was sure he'd be in trouble for drinking beer, so he planned to sneak into his bedroom and enjoy a long hot shower before facing the music. But Marion leaned out of the kitchen and greeted him cheerfully after he'd peed.

'Morning, skid,' she said and smiled. 'Thought I heard you sneaking around.'

"Sup?' Robin said weakly.

'I made fried potatoes and eggs on the electric hob if you want some,' Marion said, as Zack gurgled in the background.

Robin decided to go for hot food, because he was starved and he'd have to face Indio and Karma sooner or later. He glanced into the living room, where Finn and Otto had discovered a wall-sized projector screen and had cartoons playing way too loud.

In the kitchen, Marion was heating a bottle of formula for Zack and the washing machine was running. Karma was the only person at the big dining table, but she had on the same clothes she'd worn the night before, with bloodshot eyes and a bruised knee from an ill-advised tabletop dance.

'I know you don't like the bottle,' Marion told Zack, as the baby grizzled in his high chair. 'But Mummy was a *very* naughty girl last night and has an epic hangover.'

Karma wagged a finger and acted like she was going to tell Marion off for being cheeky, but no words came out. Robin was relieved – even if Karma remembered, she could hardly tell him off for sneaking one beer when she'd drunk so much herself.

'What about Indio?' Robin asked, scooping potatoes and eggs onto a plate and putting them in the microwave to heat up.

'Indio stumbled home about 6am and crashed out on her bed.'

'I reckon it's good that everyone danced around and went nuts,' Robin said cheerfully. 'It's been a tough few months since Designer Outlets got torched.'

'Electricity's the first good news we've had in a while,' Marion agreed, as Zack finally decided to accept the bottle of formula.

Robin took his steaming potatoes and eggs from the microwave and tried to sound casual as he sat at the dining table.

'I chatted to that refugee girl you were with yesterday lunchtime,' he said. 'She seems nice.'

'Very nice,' Marion agreed, then her eyes widened. '*That* girl you sloped off into a side room with? *That* girl you snogged?'

Robin nodded and felt his cheeks flush.

Marion licked her lips. 'You don't know her name, do you?'

'Forgot,' Robin admitted. 'It's Charlie, or Rosie or . . . One of those *ie* names.'

Marion laughed. 'Gonna be awkward next time you bump into her.'

Robin tutted. 'Just tell me.'

'I *might* be able to release that information for a modest fee.'

'I might be able to turn on a cold tap and dunk your head under it . . .'

'Her name's Josie,' Marion said as she gave Robin a big slap on the back. 'And you owe me a large burrito next market day.'

# 18. DETECTIVE HOOD

It was Saturday so school was out, but when Emma Scarlock came to the penthouse saying they were looking for volunteers to clean up the party mess, Marion told her she was looking after the baby and Robin said he needed to go help D'Angela.

Will's team had restored heat and power in the hotel rooms where everyone lived, but the lifts were still out of order, so Robin had to walk down ten floors and cross a chilly lobby and casino to reach the Nest.

'Anyone home?' Robin asked as he climbed the stairs.

He got no answer and wasn't surprised, because he'd last seen D'Angela dancing salsa with random people at two in the morning.

After testing one of the lamps in a wall socket to confirm that power had yet to reach this part of the resort, Robin climbed the ladder to the roof and was pleased to see no fresh snow on the solar panels.

The Super and all the other equipment seemed to be fine and the battery packs were at thirty per cent, which wasn't bad for a winter morning when the sun had only been up for a couple of hours.

Once Robin was satisfied that all the hardware was running, he logged in at his desk and saw that the data lake had generated several reports overnight, with sixty decrypted messages containing trigger words.

D'Angela would read them when she arrived, but Robin skimmed through quickly in case there was something that really stood out, like a message that mentioned Rex Lairde's dogs. But it all seemed routine. Robin had also done the three hacking exercises D'Angela set for him the day before.

D'Angela had accused Robin of wasting time when he started looking into the suspicious couple he'd spotted while buying his new boots, but he had nothing else to do until D'Angela rocked up, and he was still curious.

He had left the search running from the day before, and was pleased to see that the EyeZ program had found traces of Ruby Cohen-Jones in stolen databases and all over the web, from a TwoTu review of bed linen to a booking for a canal boat holiday.

Most importantly, the software had searched six hundred sets of stolen personal information. It had found eleven passwords used by Ruby Cohen-Jones and identified a meditation app on her phone with a security hole that would allow Robin to download everything stored on the device.

Robin started with Ruby's email. EyeZ logged in with no hassle, but the emails were a dull mix of online order confirmations, job applications and a sister in Australia sending endless photos of her kids.

More interestingly, Robin realised that her email account was linked to an online data back-up. The EyeZ software automatically scanned this data and flagged up an unencrypted file containing more passwords, including one for a messaging app.

Robin struck gold when he opened the messaging app. The night before Ruby's trip to the market, she'd sent a list of rare wines and vintage port to a wine merchant based in Nottingham.

After the dealer replied with an offer of £2,600 for the bottles, Ruby had messaged a friend. It seemed this friend now lived with the rebels at Sherwood Castle Resort, though frustratingly, Ruby only ever typed V instead of her full name.

By scrolling back through six weeks of messages between Ruby and V, Robin worked out that on the day Sherwood Castle Resort had flooded, Ruby had been in charge of security for the castle kitchens and dining areas.

As well as checking that customers in bars and restaurants behaved and that staff weren't pocketing tips or stealing steaks from the meat locker, Ruby held the key to a cellar containing all the most valuable booze.

So, when a wealthy customer ordered a forty-year-old whisky or a £2,000 bottle of Bordeaux, Ruby had to unlock the cellar and make sure the waiter only took the item they were supposed to.

Robin read old messages, detailing how Ruby had arranged to meet V at the Friday market and give them the key to the wine cellar. The next morning, V confirmed that he or she had opened the cellar, finding some flood damage but also plenty of valuable booze in good condition.

Over the following weeks, Ruby visited every Friday market with her husband. They'd meet V, pick up a dozen valuable bottles and sell them to the wine merchant in Nottingham.

Since the bottles were stolen and Ruby wanted cash for them, she only got a fraction of what they were worth, but she was still splitting a couple of thousand pounds per week with her husband and V.

'So, who's the mysterious V?' Robin asked himself as he logged in to the market's CCTV cameras.

Ruby and her husband hadn't been carrying anything when he saw them, so he scrolled back to the previous afternoon's footage and tracked the pair as they moved between the views from several cameras. The pair ended up cutting between two stalls at the edge of the market, where they met a woman carrying a heavy-duty shopping bag in each hand.

'Damn!' Robin gasped.

The woman had a radio headset, a holstered stun stick and one of the high-vis vests that rebel security officers wore inside the market. Robin didn't know the officer's name, but he knew her face. She'd worked for rebel security for as long as he'd been in Sherwood Forest.

Since Robin had a bounty on his back, he always carried a two-way radio so he could easily contact security. He took the little yellow handset out of his backpack and called the head of rebel security.

'Azeem, it's Robin,' he told the radio. 'Are you on duty? Over.'

'Always on duty for you, Robin,' Azeem replied cheerfully. 'What's the problem?'

# 19. FALSE PAPERS

Security chief Azeem and her sister Lyla walked upstairs to the Nest a few minutes after Robin's radio call. They'd both partied the night before, but neither drank alcohol so they'd avoided hangovers.

'Nice work, Robin,' Azeem said after she'd watched the footage. 'I'm surprised that Victoria would do something like this. She's worked with me for years.'

'Victoria needs to buy citizenship papers so her son Jordan can go to medical school,' Lyla said, defending her fellow guard. 'Costs £30,000 to bribe government officials and an immigration judge these days.'

Azeem sighed.

'Is what Victoria doing even wrong?' Lyla asked thoughtfully as she re-watched the footage in slow motion. 'The booze belonged to King Corporation, and they abandoned the castle and took a fat payout when they realised it was more profitable to claim flood insurance and shut the resort down than to repair and reopen it.'

Robin felt less satisfied with his detective work as Azeem considered their options. He knew Victoria's son Jordan from school: a gentle seventeen-year-old who was super smart and often helped Robin and Marion when they got bogged down on a maths assignment.

'Stealing booze isn't the issue,' Azeem decided finally. 'My problem is, I can't trust a security officer who's making money on the side while she's supposed to be on duty. And maybe Victoria needs money to buy her son's citizenship papers or whatever, but this community relies on people *sharing*. We should use the money from selling that booze for food and medical supplies, not just to benefit one person.'

Robin didn't know Victoria, but he kept thinking about what a nice guy Jordan was.

'Will they get kicked out of here? he asked anxiously.

'Victoria can't work security if I can't trust her,' Azeem said. 'But Victoria and Jordan have been part of our community for years. Nobody's getting kicked out.'

'Scarlock will give her a different work assignment,' Lyla added, to Robin's relief. 'Probably something unpleasant, like vermin control.'

'I'll go to the kitchens, find this locked cellar and see how much of the expensive booze is left,' Azeem said. 'Then I'll go chat to Victoria.'

'Kinda weird that nobody else found the booze,' Lyla noted.

'Kitchen is massive,' Robin pointed out. 'There's dozens of little side rooms, and all the equipment got thrown around in the flood.'

As Lyla and Azeem were about to head down the stairs, D'Angela was taking the stairs up to the Nest two at a time.

'I spoke to Will Scarlock,' D'Angela shouted, seeing that the light was on and assuming it was just Robin up there. 'We should have electricity in this part of the building in twenty minutes.'

'Nice,' Robin said as D'Angela came around the top of the stairs. 'No more standing on the roof shovelling snow off the solar panels.'

'Ahh, we have guests,' D'Angela said, surprised, then giving Robin an irritated look.

'Powerful set-up you've got here,' Azeem said after Robin had told D'Angela how he'd used the CCTV footage and EyeZ data lake to unearth Ruby and Victoria's booze-selling operation.

Lyla sounded more suspicious. 'I assume you could use this spy tech to find anyone's private info? Including mine.'

D'Angela shrugged. 'I'm only interested in finding Rex Lairde's dogs. But the answer to your question is yes. Any talented hacker backed by the resources of a government agency, or someone as wealthy as Rex Lairde, will be able to access all of your personal data.'

'I thought I'd been careful locking down my phone,' Robin added. 'But D'Angela hacked me in under a minute.'

'I've taught Robin a lot since I got here,' D'Angela told Azeem. 'The only way to totally protect data from hackers is to stick to pen and paper. But before I leave, I'll happily review your security procedures and give some advice.'

'I'd like that,' Azeem said enthusiastically, though Robin noticed her younger sister seemed less impressed. 'We'll set a date.'

Robin looked at D'Angela and smiled as Lyla and Azeem headed downstairs to the casino floor.

'Good party last night,' Robin said. 'Saw you strutting your funky stuff.'

D'Angela laughed. 'You weren't doing so bad yourself.' But her tone changed when she heard the door at the bottom of the stairs shut behind Azeem and Lyla. 'What the hell, Robin?' D'Angela hissed. 'I specifically told you not to investigate that Cohen-Jones woman any further.'

Robin looked shocked. 'You weren't here. I had nothing else to do. What harm have I done? Is Ruby working for you, or something?'

D'Angela bunched her fists and groaned with frustration. 'Ruby's not working for me. I asked you to help because you're a smart kid and you've got guts. I want to teach you some real hacking skills, but remember you're at level one, just starting out.

'There are a million things you don't understand. So when I tell you not to do something, don't do it. Especially don't do it and then invite a bunch of people in here to boast about it.'

Robin shrugged. 'I'm sorry. I didn't think it was a big deal.'

'It's Saturday,' D'Angela said. 'Go hang out with Marion and your other friends for the weekend. If I need you back on Monday, I'll let you know.'

'But I can help with the switchover when the power comes on,' Robin pleaded.

'It's just moving plugs from battery packs to wall sockets,' D'Angela said dismissively. 'I don't know if you looked at the forest map when you got here, but I've narrowed my focus to three possible settlements where I think Rex Lairde's dogs might be.'

'I guess, if you don't need me,' Robin said, so hurt that he could feel a lump in his throat.

'Who'd even want to spend all weekend in this gloomy pit with me?' D'Angela asked. 'If you like, I'll send you more hacking exercises. We can meet up and go through them tomorrow.'

Robin sighed and stood up. 'Cool. And . . . I'm sorry I ignored your instructions.'

D'Angela smiled and pointed at the staircase. 'Go have fun!'

Robin managed half a smile as he grabbed his backpack, but he felt sad as he walked downstairs, unable to figure out why D'Angela was so cross with him.

# 20. HUMAN RIGHTS

Robin feared he'd be roped into the post-party clean-up if he went back to the penthouse. Since he was frustrated with the D'Angela situation, he decided to burn off energy by hitting weights in the resort gym.

He passed the check-in desks and drained aquarium in the resort's main lobby. It was good to see no snaking queue for the showers now that people had hot water in their rooms. But as Robin got ready to hurdle the turnstile of the resort gym, Neo Scarlock called out urgently.

'Something wrong?' Robin asked.

Neo had been running, and was a touch out of breath. 'My dad wants to see you and D'Angela in his office, right now.'

'Why?'

Neo shrugged. 'He just told me to find you, then sent Lyla and Sam to get D'Angela from the Nest. I don't know what you two did, but he's not happy.'

Robin tutted. 'I didn't do *anything*.'

'My dad's not a monster,' Neo pointed out. 'Come up to the admin office and we'll sort it out.'

Will Scarlock's office was on the third floor. It had previously been the domain of Sheriff Marjorie's security chief, Moshe Klein, and was well appointed with leather sofas, a large glass desk and one wall with screens for the resort's CCTV cameras.

Klein had decorated his walls with minimalist paintings, but Will was obsessive about organising his rebel group and had replaced the art with the charts, maps and work rotas he used to keep Sherwood Castle running smoothly.

'Sit!' Will told Robin abruptly, pointing at a chair by his desk.

'Why's everyone's having a go at me today?' Robin moaned.

While most of the castle's population had spent the night partying, Will and a couple of others had kept working on restoring the vast resort's power and hot water. His blue overall was filthy from crawling around dark cupboards and mouldy floors.

Robin glanced behind as D'Angela walked in, looking defiant with Sam on one side and Lyla on the other.

'You can't treat me like this!' D'Angela spat furiously.

'This . . .' Will spluttered. 'We had a deal, D'Angela! I gave you permission to use Sherwood Castle as a base and use electronic surveillance to locate the group that kidnapped Rex Lairde's dogs. In return, you agreed to give us medical supplies and an electrical connection.'

D'Angela pointed at a blazing desk lamp. 'You got your electricity.'

'I wasn't expecting you to hack into CCTV cameras inside this castle,' Will growled. 'I wasn't expecting you to set up microphones in the weekly market, listen to everyone's mobile phone conversations, or hack the email accounts of my security officers.'

Robin gulped as he finally understood why D'Angela hadn't wanted him to share the results of his investigation with Will's security team.

D'Angela stepped closer to Will's desk, leaving Robin sandwiched between them in his chair. She paused for breath, then spoke in a firm but calm voice. 'The weekly market is a meeting point for people from all over the forest. It's an obvious intelligence-gathering location.'

Will thumped the desk, making Robin jump. 'I placed my trust in you. In return you grotesquely invaded the privacy of every single person inside Sherwood Castle Resort, and thousands of others who visited the market.'

D'Angela narrowed her eyes. 'I targeted your group because we identified it as the best organised and most trustworthy in Sherwood Forest. But Lairde will spend whatever it takes to get his dogs back, so I doubt I'll have a problem finding someone else who'll help.'

'No person shall be subject to unjustified interference with the privacy of their family, home, or correspondence,'

Will said, puffing out his chest and sounding rather pompous. 'That is a direct quote from the Universal Declaration of Human Rights.'

'The ways I track people are used by government organisations and the security departments of large corporations all over the world,' D'Angela fired back.

'So your justification for stealing people's information and invading their privacy is that it's OK because everyone else is doing it?' Will yelled, close enough for Robin to catch flying spit.

'Oh, come on!' D'Angela said. 'Don't pretend you built your rebel organisation without bending principles and breaking rules. It's how the whole world works.'

'D'Angela's teaching me heaps of stuff,' Robin interrupted. 'By the time she leaves here, our data and communications will be much more secure.'

Will and D'Angela both shot Robin *stay out of this* looks.

'If I locate those dogs, you'll have free electricity for as long as you need it and one of the wealthiest and most powerful men in the world in your debt,' D'Angela told Will. 'If you kick me out and his doggies get hurt, you will have made an extremely powerful enemy.'

Robin looked around the room as an awkward silence broke out. Sam, Neo and Lyla stood pensively at the back of the room by the double doors. D'Angela looked fiery and pissed off, while Will stared up at the ceiling, churning the awkward situation in his head.

Will hadn't been keen to deal with a ruthless businessperson like Rex Lairde and discovering that D'Angela's technique for finding his missing dogs involved stolen data and massive breaches of privacy had made him feel deceived.

But while Will wanted people's privacy respected, and feared the backlash if Forest People found out he'd allowed a billionaire to spy on them, he had to balance his morals against the grinding reality of winter weather.

'How long do you need to get this job done?' Will asked curtly.

D'Angela inhaled, giving herself time to think.

'I've narrowed my focus to three areas,' D'Angela said. 'All are recently constructed settlements of less than ten people that rarely use electronic communications. I've picked up heat signatures of dog-sized animals at all three sites, and of people sending messages using the Russian alphabet.'

'That doesn't answer my question,' Will said.

D'Angela tutted. 'A week – ten days at most.'

'I'll be generous,' Will said. 'I'll give you two weeks to finish the job. But I've had too many people asking questions about who you are and why you're here. From now on you'll avoid socialising. I'll assign a guard to escort you between the Nest and your hotel room. My son Sam will fetch your meals.'

'I can live with that,' D'Angela said. 'I'm not here to socialise.'

Will pointed at Robin. 'Now that the equipment in the Nest is running on mains electricity and you're just focused on three small settlements, I assume you can do without an assistant?'

'Agreed,' D'Angela said, despite the pleading look Robin gave her.

Will smiled at Robin. 'Which means you can go back to school on Monday, where you belong.'

Robin shook his head and mouthed *bloody hell*, but the adults ignored him.

# 21. DIBS ON THE POOL

Most forest kids had never lived in normal homes, and Robin found it hilarious watching lads who'd spent their lives caked in mud suddenly taking three hot showers a day and walking around in Sherwood Castle Resort branded bathrobes.

Marion's little brothers got addicted to putting on clothes warm from the tumble dryer and experimental cooking of everything from potatoes to chocolate bars in the penthouse microwave. They were less keen on the idea that screen-time was now set by adults, instead of watching all they could before the batteries conked out or a fuse blew.

By Sunday evening, most of the resort's power had been restored, though Will decided that lighting should be kept to a minimum. While Sheriff Marjorie and the rest of the rebels' enemies would eventually find out that they now had reliable electricity, suddenly having thousands of lights blazing into the surrounding forest was asking for trouble.

Monday was a boring and awkward return to school for Robin. D'Angela didn't get in touch, Mr Khan used every excuse to remind Robin that he was *just the same as everyone else*, and everyone seemed to know about Robin kissing Josie at the party. But instead of enjoying a blossoming romance, the pair felt shy and embarrassed and didn't know what to say to each other.

'Mr Smooth,' was Marion's sarcastic verdict after she'd witnessed it.

Tuesday was more fun because one of the resort pools had been cleaned, chlorinated and heated to a comfy twenty-eight degrees. Schoolkids were told they had dibs on the pool and afternoon lessons were cancelled for a one-off swim session.

Several parents were drafted in to give little kids swimming lessons, while older ones ran wild. Since Robin was a rubbish swimmer, he left the races and craziness to others and chilled in a black-tiled spa pool with Marion and some older kids.

'Education at its finest,' Robin joked, closing his eyes, shifting so that hot jets massaged the back of his neck, imagining that he was a million kilometres from all his troubles.

It was hard to maintain the fantasy, because at any given moment there were twenty kids screaming and twenty adults screaming at them to stop.

Josie stepped down into the jet pool, sat on the other side of Marion and started to chat. As Robin eased into their conversation, Marion's brother Otto ran past and tipped a half a bucket of cold water over Robin's head. 'How's your girlfriend, Robbo?' he squealed.

'Little turd!' Robin gasped, then ducked into the hot bubbling water.

Otto stopped running and looked back, daring Robin to chase him, but Robin waited until Otto had left before climbing out.

'What's up with you?' Marion asked as she watched him.

'Shower and get dressed before the rush,' Robin said grumpily. 'Too noisy, too many people.'

Marion smiled at Josie. 'Cheerful sod, isn't he?'

But they'd been at the pool for over an hour. Marion headed into her own posh changing cubicle, with its brass fittings and limestone floor, to get dressed. The two friends waited until it was exactly three before leaving, so Mr Khan couldn't claim that they'd skipped out before school ended.

The resort lifts now had power, but they were programmed to go nowhere without an up-to-date safety and maintenance certificate from the manufacturer. As Robin and Marion headed up the stairs to the twelfth floor, they met D'Angela coming the other way, Ten Man serving as her burly guard.

'How's it going?' Robin asked.

'Not bad,' D'Angela said as Ten Man eyed everyone suspiciously. 'I will get back to you with the solutions to my last set of hacking problems, but I've been busy.'

'Uh-huh,' Robin said, distracted because he'd realised D'Angela looked different. But also more familiar.

It was partly because D'Angela wore a singlet and baggy orange shorts, rather than the jeans and plaid shirts she'd worn when the castle was cold. But she'd also clipped her hair short.

'You know the rules,' Ten Man told D'Angela ruefully. 'No communication. Let's go.'

As D'Angela resumed walking, Robin realised he'd sounded ungrateful and called after her. 'Still loving the hacking lessons.'

'Were you staring at her boobs?' Marion accused.

'It wasn't her breasts,' Robin said, thoughtful rather than rising to Marion's bait. 'Do you remember when we saw D'Angela get out of the helicopter with Rex Lairde? I thought she was a celebrity or something, because I was sure I'd seen her face somewhere.'

'So what?' Marion said.

'Having her hair cropped has made her look even more familiar,' Robin said. 'I'm just trying to think where—'

'Your dad worked in computer security before he went to prison,' Marion suggested, as she followed Robin around another landing. 'Could he have known her?'

'Maybe . . .' Robin said, but then the answer flashed into his brain. 'Magic cheese!' he shouted.

# 22. BIG GEEKY BOOKS

'What's magic cheese?' Marion asked as Robin sped up, taking the stairs two at a time. 'Did you eat some of those mushrooms that make your brain go funny?'

'Remember that book I was reading in the summer?' Robin explained, without stopping. 'About the famous hacking group, Magic Cheese? You called me a geek every time I got it out.'

Marion smirked. 'You read a lot of geeky books.'

'There was a photo section in the middle of the book,' Robin explained. 'I think that's where I saw her.'

By the time Robin sped into the penthouse, Marion was a whole floor behind. Unfortunately, Robin's Magic Cheese book had been burned inside Designer Outlets, but it took him less than three minutes to open his laptop, log into a hacking forum and find an illegal download of the e-book.

He clicked from the book's contents page to the photo section, then flipped through pages with pictures of early hand-built hacking devices and photos of famous old-skool hackers with giant sideburns and big 1970s-style hair.

The final photo was the most recent – maybe ten years old. It was a group of five youthful hackers, with cheap booze, snack bowls and balloons on a table behind, like they were attending a naff birthday party. The only woman stood on the far left.

'That's D'Angela, right?' Robin asked Marion as he pinched to zoom in on her face. 'I'm not going mad, am I?'

'Much younger, but yeah, it's her,' Marion agreed, looking over Robin's shoulder. 'So, who is she?'

'Dasha Dudorova,' Robin said, picking the only female name from the caption below the picture. Then he read the rest of the caption aloud.

'The only known photograph of Black Bear Squad (BBS), trained by Russian intelligence and with links to the Russian mafia. BBS launched a highly sophisticated cyber-sting operation that led to the torture and imprisonment of three members of Magic Cheese by Russian agents, and the suspicious death of group founder Jason Hart.'

'Were Magic Cheese good guys?' Marion asked.

'Mostly,' Robin said, fascinated by what he'd found, but angry at D'Angela's deceit. 'Magic Cheese members stole millions by hacking banks and telephone companies, but the group was focused on stealing information and embarrassing governments on stuff like human rights abuses, pollution and corruption. They're absolute legends in the hacking community, but a lot of them wound up dead or in prison after making powerful enemies.'

'So she's Dasha Dudorova, not D'Angela Doncastro?' Marion said.

Robin nodded. 'Russian, not Argentinian.'

'You think she's a spy?' Marion suggested. 'Working for Sheriff Marjorie?'

Robin was shocked by the revelation, but his loyalties were torn. Apart from the argument over his solo investigation, he'd enjoyed D'Angela's company from the moment she'd hopped out of a helicopter and hacked his phone, while her hacking lessons had pushed his skills to a new level.

'She turned up with Rex Lairde,' Robin pointed out. 'And she really was looking for his dogs while we were in the Nest.'

'You think D'Angela's doing what she's supposed to, but hiding something about her past?' Marion suggested.

'I guess I'll have to do some more digging and try to work out what she's really up to.'

'We *have* to tell Will Scarlock,' Marion said.

Robin baulked. 'No way. He's already got it in for her.'

'Or maybe Will has good instincts and was right to be suspicious,' Marion said. 'While you're fizzing with teen boy hormones and your opinion is distorted because you like hanging out with an attractive woman who pays you lots of attention.'

'The way you keep going on about her looks, maybe it's you that fancies her,' Robin snapped back. 'Will already gave D'Angela a time limit and put her in isolation. If we show him that photo, he'll kick her out and—'

Marion finished Robin's sentence. 'We'll lose our electricity.'

'I like being warm and not having to walk down twelve floors and fight for a socket to charge my laptop,' Robin said. 'So, before Will gets involved, I need to be sure who D'Angela really is and what she's really up to.'

'Won't people on the hacking forums you use know her?' Marion suggested.

'Someone out there will know D'Angela or Dasha or whatever she calls herself,' Robin agreed. 'But she gave me this laptop, so she probably installed monitoring software on it and she's got EyeZ monitoring every bit of traffic through our internet connection.

'Hopefully me downloading the Magic Cheese book won't have tipped her off, but if I start searching for Dasha Dudorova or asking questions about her on hacking sites, she'll know what I'm up to.'

Marion groaned with frustration. 'So what do we do?'

'I guess we do it the old-fashioned way,' Robin said, grabbing his bow and a bunch of arrows. 'Look her in the eye, ask questions, and try to figure out if she's telling the truth.'

# 23. A SOCIAL VISIT

Sherwood Castle was hundreds of years old, but most of the modern resort was engulfed in stone cladding and fake turrets and had more in common with a TwoTu warehouse than a medieval relic.

Robin stood at the end of a third-floor hotel corridor and heaved mightily, trying to open a window with a half-metre snowdrift weighted against it. The frame finally swung outwards when Marion joined the effort.

After glancing back to make sure nobody could see, Robin sat on the wet window ledge and dropped a metre and a half onto the flat snow-covered roof above the casino. Marion handed bows and backpacks down to Robin before jumping herself.

It was exhausting wading through the rooftop snow, which was almost half a metre deep. After crossing the length of two football pitches, they reached the area where Robin and D'Angela had set up aerials and the now-redundant solar panels. Beyond this, the Nest was raised half a storey above, with skylights in its gently sloping roof.

Marion had been down to the casino to make sure D'Angela's guard, Ten Man, was waiting at the bottom of the stairs leading up to the Nest, but Robin still moved stealthily, creeping up to a skylight, delicately sweeping a patch of snow from the glass with the sleeve of his jacket, then peering down.

D'Angela had her bare feet propped on a desk. She tapped rapidly at a keyboard, while two big screens beyond her orange toenails showed the EyeZ-generated forest map and footage from an aerial drone.

'She alone?' Marion whispered.

Robin nodded. 'Far as I can tell. And D'Angela eats late, so I doubt Sam will bring her food any time soon.'

Robin crawled up past the skylights towards the roof hatch. There was no lock, but nor was there a handle on the outside. He'd brought a machete. Its large blade was designed for slashing through dense forest, but was also thin enough to fit into the gap around the hatch and prise it open.

He gave Marion his pack and slung his bow and two arrows over his back. 'This hatch squealed every time I came up to clear snow off the satellite dishes,' Robin explained, wedging the machete under the sill. 'You lift it up slowly, I'll drop down and take D'Angela by surprise.'

Marion knelt by the hatch, held the machete handle and levered the blade until there was an opening big enough to get her gloved fingers under.

Robin planned to drop through the hatch, glide down the outside of the metal ladder, turn deftly and point his arrow at D'Angela. Then he'd calmly but firmly order her to back away from the computers before she could yell or send a message.

But the underside of the hatch was slick with ice. Marion's hand slipped as Robin dived through the hole, and the hatch whacked him on the head. It barely hurt, but it was enough to knock him off balance.

Instead of gliding smoothly down the ladder frame, Robin tilted sideways. His bow got caught between two metal rungs and its shoulder strap briefly choked him before sliding up over his chin to set him free. He hit the floor of the Nest with a thud and a groan.

'Robin!' D'Angela gasped, running barefoot towards him. 'You lunatic! Are you OK?'

Up above, Marion had got the loft hatch open again. She thought about taking aim with her own bow and ordering D'Angela to stand still. But Robin's fall had done the job of getting her away from the computers. Though instead of the shock and awe they'd planned, D'Angela was more like a big sister, helping Robin off the floor and asking if he was hurt.

'Nice of you to drop in!' D'Angela joked, though she kept her voice low and glanced warily around to see if Ten Man had heard Robin's heavy landing. 'You OK?'

'I'll live,' Robin said. He'd scraped skin off his chin where the bow strap had slid over, but the main injury was to his pride.

'I've got a microwave now, if you fancy a hot chocolate?' D'Angela said, once she was sure Ten Man wasn't going to come up the stairs. Then she looked up at Marion. 'Come on down, you're letting the heat out with that hatch open.'

Marion and Robin exchanged awkward *what now?* glances as D'Angela poured milk into three clean mugs and stood them inside the microwave.

'Appreciate the visit,' D'Angela said, closing the microwave and dialling up four minutes. 'I'm losing my mind being alone day after day. But you guys could get in trouble, and I'd rather not do anything that sets Will off and gets me kicked out.'

D'Angela's niceness threw Robin off as he cleared his throat and tried to sound serious.

'This isn't a social visit,' he began. 'Your face looked familiar the first time I saw you. But it was only after I saw you on the stairs with cropped hair that I remembered where I'd seen you before – in a picture of a hacking group called Black Bear Squad.'

'With a caption that says your name is Dasha,' Marion added.

'And all that stuff you said about Ekoparty and growing up in Argentina was bull,' Robin said bitterly.

'I see,' D'Angela said, looking uneasy as she slid her feet into her orange Crocs. 'Does it matter who I am?'

'If you're lying about your name and where you're from, who knows what else you're lying about?' Robin said.

D'Angela smiled and switched her flawless Argentinian accent to a Russian one. 'Dasha Dudorova was a clever girl, born in a nowhere town in Russia. She excelled at languages and mathematics. She was sent to an advanced school where she learned to speak four languages fluently and became interested in computer programming, with a sideline in hacking.

'My math and language skills brought me to the attention of Russian intelligence. When I was seventeen, they tried to recruit me. I told them I had no interest in being a spy, but they were very persuasive. My twin brother was an army conscript. I was told if I didn't do what they asked, he might fall out of a helicopter in a horrible training accident. Also, that life could be made difficult for my parents and grandparents.'

D'Angela kept talking as the microwave pinged and she spooned chocolate powder into the hot milk.

'Instead of university, I was trained by the intelligence service and assigned to the Black Bear Squad. Officially we had no connection to the Russian government. But in reality, we were all trained intelligence agents, performing our patriotic duty by hacking and entrapping the enemies of Mother Russia.'

'How do I know *this* version of your life story is true?' Robin asked warily, picking up his mug.

'You don't, really,' D'Angela said.

'Does Rex Lairde know this stuff?'

'Mostly.' D'Angela nodded. 'Lairde's security people would never trust someone with my Russian intelligence background to have access to TwoTu's darkest secrets. But I'm useful dealing with special projects, like when Lairde or his company are threatened.'

'Do you still work for Russian intelligence?' Marion asked.

'No,' D'Angela said. 'I couldn't quit without consequences for my family, but I made sure my work was below average and my attitude to superiors poor. After a few years they decided I wasn't of much value and I was allowed to resign. I moved to Argentina. I changed my name to D'Angela, took a job with a local cybersecurity company, and was eventually recruited to work on special projects for TwoTu.'

'Good hot chocolate,' Marion said, inspecting the tub it had come in. 'TwoTu Peruvian Reserve Chocolate Powder.'

'I see you've both got bows,' D'Angela said. 'Are you planning to shoot me?'

'I didn't want to show Will the photo in that book before giving you a chance to explain,' Robin said, then changed the subject. 'So, are you any closer to finding Lairde's dogs?'

# 24. KNOWING THE UNKNOWABLE

'I'm sure I've found the settlement where the dogs are being held,' D'Angela said, blowing on her steaming hot chocolate as she led Robin and Marion towards the two big screens on her desk. 'But since I'm not exactly flavour of the month around here, I want to be certain before I ask Azeem to put boots on the ground.'

'What's the latest evidence?' Robin asked.

D'Angela zoomed the map until it showed a single settlement on high ground seventeen kilometres north-east of Sherwood Castle.

'It's one of the three settlements I've been looking at for a while,' she explained. 'I wasn't getting anywhere until yesterday. Everyone inside the settlement is using an encrypted data connection that I can't read, but yesterday there were two female visitors. I tracked them after they left and picked up their conversations on walkie-talkies.

'The woman was joking that the men inside were Russian geeks, who didn't use deodorant and spent all day at computers. It seems the place was a tip and the women were sent in to bring food and clean.'

'Sounds like hackers,' Robin said. 'Did they mention the dogs?'

'If they'd mentioned dogs, I would be certain and my life would be easy,' D'Angela said. 'I sent a TwoTu drone up there to take a look, but the footage didn't show anything interesting. Just a steep hillside with dense forest, blanketed in snow.'

'Drones are noisy,' Robin said. 'They might get suspicious if you send another one.'

D'Angela nodded. 'I know.'

'So, what are you waiting for?' Marion asked.

'Nothing, I guess.' D'Angela sighed. 'When you two arrived, I was checking through the data for the tenth time. I wanted to make sure I hadn't missed anything before I approach Azeem. Also . . .'

D'Angela shook her head and stopped talking.

Robin saw she looked upset and decided to push gently.

'What's the matter?' he asked.

'I read stuff about Robin Hood and Will and Emma Scarlock before I came to Sherwood Castle,' D'Angela said, reluctant, then slightly angry. 'I watched online video of the cash machine robbery you did with Marion and the archery range you shot up on Skegness Island.

'I thought I could be a mentor and teach real hacking skills to the famous Robin Hood. I knew your group had been stealing TwoTu vans for the battery packs, so I realised the thing you needed most was a reliable power supply, and I figured out a way to help you get it.

'I thought I'd be appreciated. Instead, I'm being marched in and out of the Nest like a criminal, not allowed to talk to anyone, and treated like some evil lackey for Rex Lairde and his TwoTu empire.'

Robin felt sympathetic. He knew he'd go crazy if he went days without being allowed to talk to anyone. But he also realised that a highly trained spy and hacker would know how to manipulate him to get what she wanted. And while he liked D'Angela and wanted to believe her, he had no idea if any of the stuff about her background and motivations was true.

Marion spoke as Robin got trapped in his tangled thoughts and D'Angela dabbed a tear from one eye. 'I don't know you, D'Angela,' Marion began. 'But I've known Will and Azeem my whole life. Maybe they're not your biggest fans, but they'll stick to the deal they made and help you rescue Lairde's dogs.'

Robin nodded. 'Will may have started spouting off about human rights violations, but Azeem's more interested in security than morals. She was impressed when I showed her how I'd caught Victoria shipping out the stolen booze.'

Marion nodded. 'Let's talk to Azeem first. She'll help us put a team together, so we can go check that settlement.'

'You're good kids,' D'Angela said, smiling but still a little red around the eyes. 'I never get upset like this, but it's not a nice feeling when you're out here all alone and you feel like everyone hates you.'

Robin drained his hot chocolate, picked up his bow and headed for the stairs.

'Ten Man's down there!' Marion warned.

'Roof snow killed my thighs,' Robin said. 'I'm not going back that way if I don't have to.'

Robin stepped boldly through the door at the bottom of the stairs into the casino. Ten Man shot out of a chair. 'Hey!' he shouted, then tried to grab Robin, but Robin moved too fast.

'Tell you what, Ten Man,' Robin teased as Marion and D'Angela came through the door. 'If you don't tell Will Scarlock that me and Marion snuck into the Nest, I won't tell him that we snuck past while you were asleep in your chair.'

# 25. SNOW SPEED

After studying all D'Angela's data from the settlement where she suspected the dogs were being held, Azeem agreed to lead a mission to check it out. Marion and Robin thought they'd have to put up a fight to be included, but Azeem knew that Robin's bow and climbing skills would be useful on a scouting mission, while Marion knew the forest better than anyone.

The sun was setting as the two thirteen-year-olds began the eighteen-kilometre trek, accompanied by Azeem, D'Angela and Ten Man. On a summer day it might have taken three hours, but thick snow made it hard to cross the dense forest faster than two or three kilometres per hour. While nine months in Sherwood had hardened Robin to long forest treks, D'Angela found the going tough and took a nasty slip crossing a frozen stream.

Just after nine, they reached a vast stubbly clearing left by illegal loggers. Ten Man picked up a data signal and downloaded a forecast showing blizzard conditions on the high ground they were heading towards.

'It's too risky in the dark,' Azeem said. 'We'll go again in the morning.'

The height of the skinny trees poking through the snow suggested that five or six years had passed since the illegal logging operation ended. The river the loggers had used to float timber away was frozen, but the hut they'd lived in was only missing a few planks and was mostly dry inside.

Ten Man kicked the wooden slats out of one bed frame and set them alight in the fireplace at one end of the hut. Robin and Marion snuggled up under a foil blanket on one bunk, while D'Angela cooked cans of beans and sausages in the roaring flames.

The teenagers ate hungrily and fell asleep huddled together. Azeem and Ten Man had a less restful night – they each took a four-hour shift on guard duty – while D'Angela struggled to sleep with her ankle propped on a stack of dusty pillows to stop it swelling.

'Six a.m. – let's move, move, move!' Azeem demanded, before flicking Robin's ear and tickling Marion's cheek.

The sun wouldn't come up for another two hours and the fire was out; the hut was full of groans and curling plumes of breath.

'You stink,' Marion complained, feeling Robin's arm around her back, then opening her eyes and realising that she'd turned over in the night and slept with her face in his sweaty armpit.

'Think your farts smell like jasmine and buttercups?' Robin hit back as he sat up, yawning and picking goo out of one eye.

D'Angela's ankle was puffed up to twice its normal size. Azeem suggested she stay behind, but she toughed it out with tight strapping and an anti-inflammatory jab from Ten Man's first-aid kit.

They breakfasted on Snickers bars as they began to walk. The cold made the chocolate bars so hard, they had to suck each bite for ages before it was soft enough to chew.

The last two kilometres to the settlement were over steep, rocky, ground. While a well-trodden footpath went most of the way, they couldn't use it because boot prints in the fresh snow might give their presence away.

Azeem led a brisk charge through snow-covered brush, probing with her walking stick and occasionally causing a mini-avalanche. Robin and Marion helped D'Angela, who was in agony, but whispered that she'd learned to endure pain while training for Russian intelligence.

The sky was orange with sunrise as the quartet reached a viewpoint a hundred metres uphill from the settlement, close enough for the sound of the wind battering the trees to mix with the chugging of the settlement's diesel generator.

Only the settlement's roof was visible from ground level. After a short break to share biscuits and a flask of hot tea, Robin rubbed his numb hands to prepare for a climb. He preferred the thrill of climbing trees without safety gear, but because of the wind and ice, Ten Man insisted Robin wore a safety lanyard, which he could tie at various points on the way up and which would prevent him dropping more than a couple of metres if he fell.

Slabs of snow crashed through the leafless branches as Robin expertly climbed fifteen metres. He leaned forward, snapped a couple of branches to clear his view, then let his legs dangle either side of a thick branch and raised the binoculars swinging around his neck.

Carrying building materials this deep into the forest was hard work, so most forest shelters used timber and lightweight plastic sheeting. But the two buildings Robin saw through the binoculars were built from prefabricated plastic wall sections, with solid roofs covered with corrugated metal and real glass in the windows.

The larger of the two buildings had been dug into the hillside to disguise its true size. The smaller one was open at the back, and Robin could see the exhausts of two generators, along with an insulated fuel tank and a top-of-the-range rainwater purification system.

'What have we got?' Azeem asked, using an ascender rope Robin had tied off to join him in the tree.

'They're well equipped, whoever they are,' Robin said, handing her the binoculars. 'Two generators, so there's a back-up if one goes wrong.'

'Interesting,' Azeem said, talking as she took out a thermal camera and shone it at the roof.

'They're a lot warmer in there than we are,' Robin said when he saw the red glow on the screen.

Azeem set the camera to pick out objects at human body temperature. Despite the shelter's walls, she could make out the blurry heat signatures given off by people inside.

'Six to eight people,' Azeem guessed.

'What about dogs?' Robin asked.

Azeem shook her head. 'None that I can see. But half that building is dug into the hillside and I can't get a heat signature through that.'

Down at ground level, Marion yanked Azeem's ascender rope, trying to get her attention without making a noise.

'Ten Man has spotted someone nearby,' Marion said urgently when Azeem and Robin looked down. 'Take cover.'

Robin jumped down through the branches as Azeem zipped down her rope. At ground level, there was no sign of Ten Man. D'Angela sounded worried.

'We spotted someone,' she began.

'Probably a hunter,' Marion said as she notched an arrow in her bow.

When Robin landed and grabbed his bow, there was a loud rustling that startled everyone, but it was just a large bird landing up in the tree canopy. An instant later, Robin swung his bow towards a groaning human behind trees twenty metres away.

As Marion led a charge towards the noise, the groan became a choking sound. As she closed in with her bow she saw two large men, but the dappled light between the trees made them impossible to distinguish.

One man crashed face first into the snow, unconscious. Robin and Marion ran in, aiming their bows at the guy who was still standing.

'It's me!' Ten Man said, raising his hands in the air.

Once he was sure that Robin and Marion weren't going to shoot him, Ten Man knelt in the snow, making sure his victim was unconscious before stripping a knife from the man's belt and taking the hunting rifle strapped to his shoulder.

'He was walking towards you lot,' Ten Man explained. 'I circled behind and choked him out.'

Marion and Robin only half listened, because their eyes had been drawn to the biker insignia on the back of the man face down in the snow.

'Brigands Motorcycle Club!' Robin gasped.

'My dad's gang,' Marion said. She crouched down to see the bearded face better, then realised it was a man she'd known her whole life.

# 26. ZOOT'S LOOT

Robin stepped back as he recognised Zoot, one of the most senior members of the Sherwood Forest chapter of the Brigands Motorcycle Club.

'This guy drove us back from the delta after we robbed the sneaker warehouse,' Robin explained.

Azeem looked anxiously at Ten Man. 'Did Zoot get close enough to recognise you?'

Ten Man shook his head. 'Came at him from behind.'

'Good,' Azeem said. 'Get a bag over his head before he starts coming around, tie his wrists, and everyone keep their mouths shut in case he recognises our voices.'

Zoot groaned back to consciousness as Ten Man wedged a cloth in his mouth. Robin cut two lengths of climbing rope and quickly tied Zoot's wrists and ankles. Finally, Ten Man yanked Zoot's thick body warmer up over his head and zipped it tight so he couldn't see.

'What a mess,' Azeem hissed as everyone backed away from Zoot.

'I don't understand,' D'Angela said.

Azeem began by pointing at Marion. 'Marion's father is Jake "Cut-Throat" Maid, leader of the Sherwood Forest chapter of the Brigands Motorcycle Club. They're one of the largest and most powerful bandit groups in the forest. While we don't agree with everything the Brigands do, we cooperate in many areas and keep our noses out of the rest.'

D'Angela nodded. 'And Ten Man choked out one of their guys, which they won't be happy about.'

'They're volatile,' Marion explained. 'I love my dad, but the Brigands are this big macho brotherhood. They swear an oath that if you disrespect one member, the whole gang is duty bound to get revenge.'

'A beef with the Brigands is the last thing I need,' Azeem said, sounding stressed.

D'Angela spoke thoughtfully. 'We picked up heaps of surveillance from the Brigands. I saw nothing to indicate that they were involved with Russian mafia or a sophisticated kidnapping plot.'

'My dad's people lost their bikes, their camp and everything else in the summer floods,' Marion explained. 'They're flat broke, but everyone's still scared of them . . .'

D'Angela nodded. 'So Zoot and some other Brigands are working up here as hired muscle?'

'Exactly,' Marion said.

'OK . . .' D'Angela said, then gently clapped her gloved hands. 'We're pretty sure Zoot didn't recognise anyone before Ten Man choked him out. So, we make it look like he was jumped and robbed by bandits. Steal his wallet, his weapons, give him a black eye. While you do that, I'll hack Zoot's phone. When he crawls back to the settlement, his phone will be sending me live audio and video of everything that's going on inside.'

'Nice,' Robin said admiringly.

'Wouldn't robbers steal his phone, though?' Marion asked.

'True,' D'Angela said.

'Make a big scratch in the screen and leave it on the ground nearby,' Robin suggested. 'It'll still work, but Zoot will figure that the robbers didn't bother taking a broken phone.'

'Clever boy,' D'Angela said, putting her hands on her hips and cracking a big smile. 'You thought that up on the spot?'

Robin grinned and looked flattered. 'I'm even smarter than I look.'

Marion tutted. 'That's not hard . . .'

Azeem seemed happy with the plan and took charge again. 'How long to hack Zoot's phone?'

'Six minutes,' D'Angela said. 'Ten, tops.'

'Go get the phone,' Azeem said. 'Marion, strip Zoot of valuables. Ten Man can give him a black eye.'

'I've got morphine in the medical kit,' Ten Man said. 'That'll make sure he doesn't come round for a bit.'

'We can't risk that in this cold,' D'Angela said. 'Hypothermia could set in within twenty minutes, and we're not trying to kill the guy. In fact, we probably need to fire a gun or something to make sure the others come looking for him.'

'What do I do?' Robin asked, staying back as Ten Man pinned Zoot under his boot, Marion stripped him of his watch and D'Angela fished his phone from the back of his jeans.

'Get back up the tree,' Azeem ordered. 'Let us know if anyone comes in or out of the settlement.'

But D'Angela completed the hack before Robin was even halfway up.

'You're all dead!' Zoot growled as he managed to spit his gag. Then Ten Man's huge fist delivered a black eye. Zoot groaned.

D'Angela scratched up Zoot's hacked phone and dropped it lightly in the snow alongside him, Robin packed away the climbing gear around the tree, and Azeem fired two shots into the trees with the stolen hunting rifle.

The blasts sent a satisfying echo down the hillside and Zoot's cursing and yelling made everyone sure that he'd be found before the cold did him serious damage.

'Fast as you can,' D'Angela said, trying to ignore the pain in her foot as they raced off. 'At least it's downhill this way.'

# 27. IT'S COMPLICATED

The scout party got back to the castle just before midday. After warming up with hot showers, then a lunch of spaghetti and meatballs, Will Scarlock called Robin, Marion and D'Angela in for a meeting. Azeem had already been in and explained the Zoot situation.

'I'm sorry,' Will began. Azeem and D'Angela sat by his desk, while Robin and Marion stood behind. 'The electricity and medical supplies Rex Lairde has supplied us with have made a huge difference to our quality of life. But there's a delicate balance of power in the forest between ourselves, the New Survivors, the Brigands and the other large groups. I often disagree with things they do, but the forest is big enough for us to co-exist without getting in each other's way.

'I know part of my agreement with Rex Lairde was that we'd help rescue his dogs once you'd located them. But I believed they were being held by a Russian mafia group—'

'They are,' D'Angela interrupted. 'Almost all the communications I picked up around that settlement are in Russian.'

Will nodded. 'There's a difference between a Russian mafia group acting alone and a Russian mafia group using Brigands to provide extra security. We provide food, shelter and medical care to hundreds of Forest People every week, especially in this bitter weather. If we get into a violent dispute with the Brigands, that will be jeopardised.'

'But Marion said the Brigands lost everything,' D'Angela said hopefully. 'If I arrange to pay them off, we won't have a problem.'

Marion shook her head. 'The Brigands and most other bike gangs have a rule they call *blood for blood*,' she explained. 'Once you physically hurt a biker, it's a blood feud. You can't buy them off, no matter how much money you offer.'

'Seriously?' D'Angela said, gawping. 'That's crazy.'

'Blood for blood means a situation can turn violent very quickly,' Marion said. 'But people are scared to start a fight with a biker when they know the rest of the gang will defend him, no matter what.'

Will sighed. 'Even if Rex Lairde's money could buy off the Brigands, the Russian mafia wouldn't be happy. You might end up with a war between the Brigands and Russian gangsters – and if people realise we were involved, we'd get dragged into it too.'

'Surely locating the dogs was the difficult part,' Azeem said, looking at D'Angela. 'With Rex Lairde's resources, you can hire a team of professionals to do the rescue job. Soldiers, ex-special forces or whatever.'

'But Lairde will cut our electricity,' Robin complained. 'I don't want to go back to freezing my arse off all day.'

Will eyed Robin, sounding cross. 'We cannot afford a war with the Brigands, Robin. Speaking of which, are we absolutely certain Zoot didn't recognise any of you?'

D'Angela answered. 'We hacked Zoot's phone, turning it into a listening device. We listened in when the Russians found him and they seemed sure he'd been tied up and robbed by random bandits.'

'That's a relief,' Will said.

'What other info have you picked up from inside the settlement?' Azeem asked.

'I know who's in there,' D'Angela said. 'Four Russians, plus Zoot and another Brigand providing security.'

'We haven't heard any barking or a mention of Lairde's dogs, though,' Robin added, sounding curious.

D'Angela shot Robin an angry look, then tipped back her head and surprised everyone by sobbing. 'You won't hear any dogs because they're not in the forest!'

Robin looked baffled. 'What?'

'Why would Rex Lairde invent a story about his dogs being kidnapped?' Azeem asked. 'Has he got some other beef with the Russian mafia?'

'It's complicated,' D'Angela said, as she smudged a tear from under one eye. 'I have the beef with the Russian mafia, not Rex Lairde.'

Will got off his chair and put his palms flat against the desktop. 'But you work for Lairde. He flew out here with you. I met him.' He sounded irritated.

'I wanted to help you guys because I admire the way you all help refugees and fight for justice,' D'Angela explained. 'I also needed Lairde's resources to sort some issues I have with the Russian mafia, but after working at TwoTu for a few years I realised that the only thing Rex Lairde cares about is his mop dogs.'

'I'm lost,' Robin admitted. 'Did Lairde's dogs get kidnapped or not?'

'The dogs got kidnapped,' D'Angela said. 'But it was me that did it.'

# 28. BROTHER AND LOVER

'I'll go back to the beginning and try to explain,' D'Angela said, as Marion, Robin, Will and Azeem stared at her with a mix of irritation and curiosity. 'Some of you already know that my real name is Dasha Dudorova and I'm from Russia, not Argentina.

'My twin brother Pytor and I were brainy kids who developed an interest in computers and hacking. At seventeen we both got recruited by the Russian intelligence service. We didn't want to leave home, but we'd done some stuff that was illegal, so the alternative was getting our heads shaved and a one-way ticket to a prison colony.

'In training we met Ivan. He became my boyfriend and my brother's best friend. Pytor and Ivan were competitive, and our instructors encouraged that rivalry to make them excel at whatever they did.

'I was as talented as my brother, but I wanted to get out. I deliberately did mediocre work and started arguments with my superiors. Being sexist middle-aged men, they decided I was a crazy hormonal woman who was no use as a hacker, and they let me leave.

'Ivan and Pytor stayed and got promoted. But while hackers are useful to governments, one talented hacker can make millions, even billions, for criminals. Then they both disappeared. I was told they were on a secret mission. But I still had contacts inside the intelligence service and I found out that they had been sold to a criminal gang – as if they were cattle.'

'I read rumours about this stuff on the dark web,' Robin said. 'Hackers forced to work by organised crime groups. Beaten and starved if they don't do what they're told.'

D'Angela was pleased to see the confused, cynical faces around her become more sympathetic. 'When people think of slavery, they tend to think about domestic staff or factory workers. But it can happen to professional people too – doctors forced to work for warlords, chemists kidnapped to make illegal drugs, computer experts forced to hack.'

'Awful,' Marion said.

D'Angela continued her story. 'I started my new life in South America, but kept a close eye on the Russian hacking community, listening for any rumours about gangs that used people like Ivan and Pytor. I didn't get anywhere until the start of this year. I identified computer code that had been used to hack a TwoTu payment server. My brother must have found out that I was working for

TwoTu, because when we found the Trojan software used for the attack, its filename was a password my brother and I had used at a local web café when we were kids.

'It wasn't much of a clue, but using TwoTu's resources I traced the source of the code and worked out that Ivan and Pytor were hacking for a Russian money-laundering operation based in Sherwood Forest.

I knew they would be deep in the forest, and well guarded, so I needed TwoTu's money and resources to stand any chance of rescuing them. Around the same time, I started seeing stories in the news about Robin Hood and the rest of you guys sticking it to Guy Gisborne and Sheriff Marjorie. I began working on a plot that would not only free Ivan and Pytor, but help you guys too.

'First, I worked out how to access Lairde's Capital City penthouse and steal his precious dogs. I knew he'd use me to help find them, because the cops and Forest Rangers around here are so corrupt.'

'So instead of looking for the dogs, you were spending Lairde's money looking for your brother?' Marion asked.

'And trying to help us too?' Robin added.

'That was my grand plan,' D'Angela said, nodding.

'I'm still not comfortable with the way you invaded everyone's privacy,' Will said. 'But if what you're saying is true, I should have treated you with more respect.'

'If,' Azeem said pointedly. 'I don't mean to be rude, D'Angela, but how do we know this story is any truer than the ones you've told us before?'

'I did hear those names – Ivan and Pytor – through Zoot's bugged phone,' Robin said.

'I understand that I've put you in a difficult position with the Brigands,' D'Angela said. 'Since I've been at Sherwood Castle, I've watched refugees arriving frozen and half starved. I've seen how important the market is to all Forest People, as well as Dr Gladys's clinic and Sheila's chickens and the free internet access, and I've met the law students you bring in to give immigration advice. I can't ask you to risk a war with the Brigands and put everything you've built in jeopardy. I'll have to find a different way to rescue Ivan and my brother.'

'I *want* to help you,' Robin said firmly, and Marion nodded in agreement.

D'Angela smiled. 'Rex Lairde's dogs are being looked after by a friend of mine. I'll tell Lairde you helped me rescue them and you'll keep your electricity.'

'We'd be grateful for that,' Will said.

Azeem nodded before speaking. 'As head of security, I can't get involved in any operation that might put us in conflict with the Brigands. Nor can Ten Man or any of my other security officers. But I can supply any equipment you need, and I can probably find trustworthy people who can help you.'

'And you can keep your surveillance gear set up in the Nest until your brother and boyfriend are free men,' Will added.

'I've funnelled some of Lairde's money into accounts I control,' D'Angela said. 'It's not a fortune, but anyone who helps rescue Ivan and my brother will be decently paid.'

'In my opinion, you should move quickly with any rescue operation,' Azeem said. 'The faster you act, the less chance there is of information leaking out and your brother being moved to another location.'

Marion made an *umm* sound before speaking with an unusual lack of confidence. 'I'm . . . in touch with someone who might help with the rescue,' she began, before pausing awkwardly. 'They're tough, and desperate for money. They're a little reckless, but they've lived in the forest their whole life. They can handle weapons and they're not closely associated with us.'

'Sounds ideal to me,' D'Angela said brightly.

Azeem sounded more suspicious. 'Who are we talking about here?'

'My brother, Flash,' Marion said.

# 29. ENJOY THE TRIP

'Good luck,' Azeem told D'Angela as she headed purposefully out of Will's office. Marion and Robin marched behind her.

'Flash is a cool guy,' Robin told D'Angela urgently as he walked. 'But the last time I went out with him, his supposed girlfriend Agnes betrayed us. I almost got shot and I wound up drenched in neon-pink sludge.'

'Agnes is still his girlfriend,' Marion said they walked towards a curved staircase leading down to the casino floor. 'They kissed and made up.'

'What?' Robin gasped. 'Agnes is a psycho. And when did you get back in touch with Flash?'

'Ages ago, before the fire.'

'You didn't tell me,' Robin said, offended.

Marion snorted. 'Because you have a big mouth.'

'Hey!'

'Look, I know that Flash and Agnes aren't perfect,' Marion said. 'But they know the forest. They're tough, they need money, they know how to handle weapons, and if I call Flash I bet he'll get here in a few hours.'

'I still don't trust them,' Robin said. 'Azeem said she could find someone to help us. I think we should ask her for a recommendation.'

Marion shrugged. 'At least we know Flash. If Azeem recommends people we don't know, can we trust them not to take the money and leg it when the shooting starts?'

They had reached the bottom of the stairs. The trio set off across the thick casino carpet towards the Nest.

'First, if we plan this right, we'll take the settlement by surprise and there shouldn't be any shooting,' D'Angela said. 'Second, am I right in thinking that the Brigands are led by Cut-Throat Maid, who is Marion and Flash's father?'

'He's our dad,' Marion confirmed.

D'Angela smiled. 'If trouble breaks out, do you think Zoot will attack the son and daughter of his gang's leader?'

Robin laughed. 'The last time I heard Cut-Throat speak about Flash, he said he'd drown him in a sewage pit if he ever saw him again.'

'But would Cut-Throat *really* do that?' D'Angela asked, then looked at Marion. 'And what if he finds out you were involved in a raid that went against two of his own people?'

'My dad acts tough,' Marion said. 'He'd stamp and scream and threaten me with all kinds of terrible punishments. But I'll always be Daddy's little girl.'

'Useful to know,' D'Angela said as they walked swiftly past the rows of silent slot machines. 'Though if we get this right, the bad guys won't see our faces before we take them out.'

'I want it on record that I think using Flash and Agnes is a mistake,' Robin said sternly.

'Noted,' D'Angela said, then looked at Marion. 'Give this brother of yours a call. Tell him to get here as fast as he can. Make sure he arrives through a side entrance and stays out of sight.'

'Will do,' Marion said, sticking out her tongue at Robin before pulling out her phone.

'Are you *sure* you know what you're doing?' Robin asked.

D'Angela laughed. 'I don't know Sherwood Forest and I might not be as fit as I was ten years ago, but Russian intelligence puts everyone through some pretty tough military training. Even geeks like me, who sit in front of a computer.'

'If Robin doesn't like it, he doesn't have to come,' Marion teased. 'In fact, he's more recognisable than anyone. He's probably a liability.'

'Get stuffed!' Robin growled furiously. 'I'm not missing the action, even if that idiot Flash—'

D'Angela hooked Robin's ankle, gave him a shove, then grabbed the back of his T-shirt to make sure he landed gently on the soft carpet. Almost simultaneously, she pushed Marion towards a video poker machine, then spoke with her thickest Russian accent. 'Games and teasing stop now!' she said, snapping her fingers dramatically. 'We are a team. We work together, but I am in charge. If either of you don't like that, quit now and get out of my sight.'

There was a pause. Robin got up from the floor, looking a little shocked, and Marion untangled herself from between two stools in front of the poker machine.

'Seems you're both still here,' D'Angela said. 'Marion, go to the Nest and make that phone call. Robin, head for the animal sheds out back and grab tranquilliser guns and as many darts as you can carry.'

# 30. EVERYONE, IT'S FLASH

Flash told Marion he was knackered and couldn't get to the castle before the following morning. Since they would face a repeat of their gruelling uphill hike to the settlement, D'Angela decided it was better if they all got a good night's sleep anyway.

At sunrise, Robin, Marion and D'Angela crept out the back of Sherwood Castle Resort, crossing an overgrown golf course and entering a flood-damaged greenkeeper's hut where Flash and Agnes were waiting.

'Good morning, Kevin,' Marion said, using the real name her big brother hated as she pulled him into a hug. 'I hate to admit it, but I've missed you.'

Agnes sat on a chair behind a woodworking bench. Robin thought she looked evil with her scarred cheek and beady eyes. They exchanged scowls.

'What happened to your curls?' Robin asked Flash as the muscular seventeen-year-old slapped him on the back.

'Cops are after me,' Flash said. 'Been working at one of Gisborne's trash dumps in Locksley, so I had to change my look.'

'A real job!' Marion said, aghast.

D'Angela made a more formal introduction and shook Flash's hand. Agnes got out of her chair as D'Angela reached across the bench to shake hers, and Robin gawped as he saw the swollen belly beneath Agnes's winter coat.

'What the zippity-doo-dah?' Marion gulped.

Flash gave a cheeky smile. 'You're gonna be an auntie, Marion. We've both got false identity papers. The wedding's booked for the day I turn eighteen.'

'A marriage that will surely span the decades,' Robin scoffed, shaking his head in horror.

D'Angela had more practical concerns. She scowled at Flash. 'You didn't mention that she's pregnant.'

'I know there's three of us,' Flash said. 'But I'm still only charging for two.'

'I'm only five months gone,' Agnes snapped. 'I'm not an invalid. I've been running and lifting weights every day.'

Robin thought there was going to be a row, but D'Angela swallowed her anger, grabbed her furry hat and headed for the door.

'We don't have much gear,' Flash noted as they stepped outside and picked up their packs.

'There's an abandoned logging site two-thirds of the way there,' D'Angela said. 'We'll travel light. TwoTu drones will meet us there with extra equipment, food and water.'

'And our cash?' Flash asked.

'Ten thousand each, as agreed,' D'Angela said while Robin and Marion pulled on their backpacks. 'Five when we get to the clearing. Five when we complete the operation.'

Agnes tutted. 'Rex Lairde's a zillionaire. We could have got ten times that.'

Flash scowled at his pregnant girlfriend and the somewhat unhappy band set off over the snowy golf course. Marion led the way, since she knew the forest and had done the hike two nights earlier. With daylight and clear skies on their side, it took less than three hours to reach the loggers' hut where they'd slept last time.

While D'Angela connected to the internet with a satellite phone and listened to the latest recordings from Zoot's hacked mobile, Robin and Marion went outside, just as two beefy TwoTu drones landed in the clearing.

Robin and Marion jogged over to them and used hunting knives to release the heavily padded cargo boxes slung beneath the four propellers. As well as £40,000 in cash, there was stuff like electrical ties, stun guns, earpiece radios and masks for the raid, plus a generous supply of new arrows.

D'Angela had also ordered a luxury picnic hamper, with tablecloth, plates and cutlery. Inside was a swanky lunch of Irish stew kept hot in a big vacuum flask, fresh bread, cheese, sliced meats, salmon pâté, fruit juice and a fresh cream gateau. It had got a little bashed up on the drone flight, but still tasted delicious.

D'Angela's Russian instructors had taught her that sharing good food was an excellent way for a team to bond quickly. She was pleased when Flash, Marion and Robin joked and laughed together, reminiscing about stuff they'd been through. Only Agnes remained aloof, holding her nose and moaning that she hated fish and that pregnant people can't eat mouldy cheese.

After the plates and bowls had been cleared from the table, D'Angela set a large-screen tablet in the middle of the table to give them all a final briefing. She showed everyone photos of the people inside the settlement, along with a bunch of information that EyeZ had dug up on each of them.

'We're here to rescue these three,' D'Angela explained. 'My brother Pytor and his friend Ivan. The third guy is called Mads. I haven't been able to unearth his background, but he's being treated like a captive and seems friendly with my brother.

'The three hackers are being guarded by four bad guys. Two are Brigands, Zoot and Insane Rob. They do the cooking and provide extra security when the guys running the operation leave the settlement.

'The bosses are Russian mafia, Novel and Alexi. I've dug up information about their criminal pasts and the gang they work for. The important thing to note is that they're both former Russian intelligence officers, so expect them to be cunning and don't believe a word that comes out of their mouths.

'They're also thoroughly nasty pieces of work. Over the last couple of days, I've heard them slap and punch Pytor when he made a mistake, and threaten Ivan and Mads with electric shocks.

'Now, this last leg of the hike is uphill, and should take a couple of hours. I remind you that it's *vital* none of us get recognised by Zoot and Insane Rob. We'll put on gloves, helmets and face masks when we get within a kilometre of the settlement. Try not to speak during the operation, but if you have to, remember that the less you say, the less chance there is of someone recognising or remembering your voice.

'Lastly, Robin, you're famous enough to be recognised even under a mask, so stay back. Cover us with your bow and leave close-range stuff to us unless you have no choice.'

Robin tutted and sighed, though he knew it made sense.

'Is all of that clear?' D'Angela asked.

As everyone around the table said yes or nodded, she pulled packets of cash sealed in cling wrap from one of the drone cargo boxes and threw one to everyone.

'Five thousand each,' D'Angela said as Robin opened his envelope and stared happily at his money. 'Don't do anything stupid or you might not get to spend it. Now let's get the hell out of here.'

# 31. SHOOTIN' TIME

The winter weather had been merciful. The afternoon sun warmed the backs of the party of five as they stopped close to where Ten Man had ambushed Zoot two days earlier. As Robin climbed a tree to carry out a visual check, D'Angela listened to the live feed from Zoot's bugged phone.

The plan was to lure the Russians and Brigands outside rather than storm the main hut and risk a shootout. D'Angela reckoned the best way to kick off was to damage the external generator that provided electricity, but hearing a gunshot or finding an arrow sticking out of the fuel tank would tip the bad guys off, so someone had to get up close to do it.

Flash and Marion donned masks, gloves and earpiece radios as they closed in on the rear of the settlement. D'Angela went around to cover the front. Robin found himself feeling awkward as he went to a side position with a good view and wound up crouching in snowy bushes next to Agnes.

He watched through binoculars as Marion grabbed the foam-insulated fuel hose between the diesel tank and the low building that connected the two generators and water purification unit. D'Angela had seen or heard nothing to indicate that the bad guys had CCTV cameras, but she still carefully listened to the live audio from Zoot's bugged phone as Flash pulled out an awl, designed for making holes.

It would have been faster and easier to slash the pipe, but they didn't want the sabotage to look obvious. Marion held the flexible pipe taut as Flash peeled back the foam insulation and gouged a couple of holes. As Marion stepped back to avoid splashes of trickling diesel, the bright yellow generator spluttered to a halt.

D'Angela listened to the men in the hut curse and moan about the power going out. As Marion and Flash did their best to sweep away their footprints and hide behind the nearest trees, the beanpole-thin Russian – called Alexi – came out of the main hut's front door, hurriedly pulling on a thick jacket.

'Fuel pipe!' Alexi yelled when he saw the diesel puddling in the snow. 'Mads, find some heavy-duty tape and get out here.'

Mads stepped out, a small Scandinavian-looking guy with straight blond hair and green eyes. He only wore a lightweight hoodie, and he slipped about in the snow in his flimsy pool shoes. He clearly hadn't seen daylight in a while, because he kept one hand over his face to shield his eyes from the brightness of the sun reflecting off the snow.

'I need sunglasses,' Mads said, struggling to inspect the leaking pipe.

Alexi showed zero sympathy, bunching a fist and growling, 'Get on with it.'

Mads's socks were soon soaked in snow and fuel. He flipped open a control panel on the side of the fuel tank and turned a red valve to stop the leak.

D'Angela sent an order through her earpiece. 'It's all clear at the front. Time to take those two out.'

Marion was less than five metres from her target. She leaned out from behind a tree trunk, took careful aim and shot a tranquilliser dart at Alexi's bum.

The dart was designed for animals like bears and horses, that are three or four times heavier than humans. D'Angela's research suggested the tranquilliser gun and darts Robin had found in the animal sheds would knock a man out instantly but would do no lasting damage. Unfortunately, Marion hadn't shot the dart through Alexi's jeans, but into the fat leather wallet he kept in his back pocket.

'What the hell?' Alexi shouted, spinning around and seeing the dart drop to the ground.

Mads had no idea that the shooters were here to rescue him. He panicked, diving into the snow and blinding himself when leaked fuel splashed into his eyes. Mads screamed in pain and Marion reloaded her dart gun, and

Alexi sprinted back to the main door screaming, 'We're under attack!'

Robin took a clear shot. Alexi snowploughed forward, a tranquilliser-tipped arrow buried in his thigh. D'Angela watched the front door of the main hut, hoping that the other Russian or one of the two Brigands would come out to save Alexi, but instead the heavy door slammed and a metal bolt clanked across the inside.

Flash and Marion were close enough to hear Zoot shouting inside the hut. 'The bandits who robbed me are back! Get the guns.'

'Be careful!' Agnes shouted to her boyfriend without thinking as Flash charged up to the side of the hut. He smashed the side window with a hefty branch. Marion followed two steps behind, pulling the pins on a pair of smoke grenades and dropping them through the window.

They heard swearing and shouts inside the hut as the smoke erupted. Marion and Flash ducked as someone blasted a shotgun towards the window from inside. Flash lobbed a third smoke grenade to add to the torment before backing away.

Then a hatch opened on the hut roof.

'Roof!' Agnes shouted.

The Russian gangster, Novel, pulled himself out through the hatch, followed by a gasping Zoot and plumes of smoke.

Robin had another clear shot. He took Novel down with a tranquilliser shot between the shoulders as he tried to jump off the roof. Robin swung his bow towards Zoot, but Marion took him out from below with a tranquilliser dart to his flabby gut.

As Zoot's huge frame flopped, unconscious, across the snowy metal roof, D'Angela saw her brother Pytor. He was coughing violently as he opened the window on the other side of the hut and tried to climb out.

'Sister!' he shouted in Russian, as D'Angela grabbed him under the armpits to help him through.

That just left Insane Rob and Ivan inside the smoke-filled hut. Everyone could hear the pair's hacking coughs. Flash reckoned they were close to passing out as he moved around to the front door. He tried to kick it open, but the sliding bolt on the inside was solid.

Agnes slid a long-handled axe from her backpack, slamming Robin sideways. He half expected her to betray him, like she'd done a few months earlier, knocking him out while everyone was distracted and dragging him away to claim the bounty on his head, but Agnes bravely hurtled down the snowy slope towards the hut with her big axe and pregnant belly.

While Flash and Marion tried to break the metal door off its hinges, Agnes was smarter and swung her axe two-handed into the lightweight panels that made up the side of the building. The plastic shattered when Agnes ripped the axe out, exposing thick silver insulation and wisps of smoke.

'He might shoot,' Flash warned, scared for his pregnant girlfriend, but realising it was easier to tear out a plastic wall panel than a metal door.

Flash barged Agnes aside, grabbed her axe and took another swing. Pent-up grenade smoke spewed through the new hole, forcing Flash and Agnes to back off. Robin covered them with his bow, but nobody came out.

When the smoke had cleared enough for them to look inside, Flash saw Insane Rob on the floor, close to the shotgun but choking on smoke and clearly too weak to pick it up.

'Dart!' Flash ordered.

Marion ducked inside and shot the Brigand in his big belly with a tranquilliser dart.

'Ivan, we're here to help you,' Marion shouted, then held her breath as she stepped into the hut and looked around for the last man.

The front door bolt clanked and Ivan stumbled out, half blind, with a wet rag over his face and a string of snot dripping off his chin. He sighted the girlfriend he'd not seen in six years and forgot all his injuries.

'Dasha, Dasha, Dasha!' Ivan boomed, opening his arms and stumbling towards her.

Robin's eyes flooded with tears as D'Angela embraced Ivan and Pytor. As they sobbed and babbled in Russian, Robin felt the happiest he'd been in ages. As he stumbled downhill from his cover position to join the celebration, he knew he'd done a good thing.

# 32. NO KILLING TODAY

Ivan and Pytor were OK once they'd drunk some water and let their eyes adjust to the daylight, but Mads was still blind after going face down in the spilled fuel. Robin took a chair from inside the hut and she sat on it while he used lots of water to flush his stinging mouth and red, painful eyes.

The rest of the team worked swiftly on a clean-up. Zoot and Insane Rob were unconscious and mostly uninjured. Flash stripped their pockets, fitted them with hoods and dragged them clear of the site while D'Angela and Agnes pulled the two Russians in the opposite direction.

'We should put bullets in their heads,' Pytor said bitterly, spitting at his former captors. 'They treated us like slaves for five years.'

'They pushed my head in a filthy toilet,' Ivan added. 'Because I asked for one day off when I was sick.'

'We're not killing anyone today,' D'Angela said ruefully. 'We'll tip the Brigands off so they can come for their men.'

'They only gave us slippers, to make it harder for us to escape,' Pytor said. 'So we'll take their boots. With any luck, they'll get frostbite.'

Only wisps of smoke remained in the hut when Pytor and Ivan went inside. They gathered their few personal possessions, money and some warm clothes that had belonged to their captors, and took some valuable items, including a laptop and back-up drives with lots of data on their most recent hacks and the illegal activities they'd been forced to take part in.

Pytor, Ivan and Mads hadn't been outdoors in months. Their sense of wonder at being free and breathing fresh air briefly energised them, but they were unfit after being held captive for so long, and the boots they'd taken from their captors were a poor fit – especially for Mads, who was the smallest of the three but had drawn the short straw and wound up wearing a pair of giant biker boots, fresh off Zoot's stinking feet.

D'Angela and Agnes started the next leg of the journey, walking towards the top of the hill to the north with the former captives, while Robin, Marion and Flash stayed back. They filled buckets with fuel and splashed it around inside the huts, then Flash ripped the pipe off the big diesel tank so that the surrounding area flooded too.

Marion complained that she hadn't blown anything up in ages, so Robin lit a flaming arrow and filmed on his phone as she shot it fifty metres over the treetops into the fuel-soaked remains of the settlement.

'Toasty!' Robin said as the roof of the main hut flew up, doing pirouettes, tailed by flames jetting ten metres into the air.

The local bird population didn't seem impressed, but the trio felt good as they jogged to catch up with D'Angela, Agnes and the slow-moving former captives. After marching to the top of a steep hill they walked two kilometres along a ridge and allowed Mads, Ivan and Pytor to catch their breath with a stop at a former television transmission station.

The giant transmission mast had been melted for scrap, but a small brick structure about the size of a school classroom remained, with a partly collapsed roof and racks of rusted radio equipment.

Rats shot in every direction as they stepped through the door, which hung off its hinges. The former captives found three grubby plastic chairs to sit on and D'Angela set her pack on a mildewed wooden table.

After handing everyone chocolate bars and cartons of apple juice, she pulled out four envelopes with five thousand pounds in each.

'This is where we go our separate ways,' D'Angela said, sounding emotional as she slid packets of cash across the table to Flash, Agnes, Robin and Marion. 'This doesn't seem like enough when I think about what it means to have Ivan and Pytor back.'

'I'd have to work six weeks at Gisborne's trash dumps to earn this much,' Flash said keenly as he opened his packet and fanned the notes. 'It'll buy all the stuff we need for the baby.'

'Why aren't you going back to Sherwood Castle?' Agnes asked.

'We have to get out of the forest,' D'Angela explained. 'I'm sure the Brigands and mafia dudes didn't get a chance to identify you guys, but they will be looking for Mads, Ivan and Pytor. I've booked a car to pick us up near Route 9. We'll lie low at a friend's house for a couple of days while the boys get their strength back, then we'll head east to the delta. Robin put me in touch with a smuggler pal down there who'll find a boat to take us out of the country.'

'Are you OK for money?' Marion asked, pocketing her cash.

D'Angela nodded. 'TwoTu paid me well these past few years. I'm not rich, but I've got enough to get us out of the country. Wherever we end up, I'm sure four ace hackers will find a way to make a living.'

Then D'Angela looked fondly at Robin. 'I guess the Nest is your hacking den now,' she began. 'It's a pretty impressive rig for a thirteen-year-old.'

Robin smiled. 'Won't Lairde want his kit back?'

D'Angela shook her head. 'TwoTu make billions. They're not gonna send people out into the forest to retrieve used computer gear worth £30,000.'

'And you're quitting TwoTu?' Marion asked.

D'Angela nodded. 'I only took the job because it meant I could get my hands on the resources I needed to find

Ivan and Pytor. I hate the way big businesses like TwoTu operate. Also, Lairde employs a lot of smart people. I don't want to be around if one of them figures out it was me that kidnapped his precious doggies.'

'I've really enjoyed your hacking lessons,' Robin said sadly.

He'd grown to like D'Angela, but in minutes she'd be heading off north, he'd go back to Sherwood Castle and they'd likely never see each other again.

D'Angela realised Robin was sad and smiled. 'Once I get settled, you can expect some extra-tough hacking challenges delivered to your inbox.'

'Cool,' Robin said, battling tears as he stood up to give D'Angela a goodbye hug.

While D'Angela had been speaking, Mads, Pytor and Ivan had been jabbering in Russian. Pytor stood and interrupted D'Angela before Robin got his embrace.

'There's something to discuss before we split,' Pytor said, speaking excellent English but without his sister's talent for masking her Russian accent. 'Something we can do together. It will hurt the scumbags who stole my freedom – and will make all of us a *lot* of money.'

# 33. HERE'S PLAN B

Flash and Agnes perked up at the mention of money. D'Angela didn't look happy, but let her brother keep talking.

'Most of the hacking work we've been doing in the forest is related to money laundering,' Pytor explained. 'Criminals have to show where the money they spend comes from. Our job was to hack banks and government systems and make it look as if money earned through robberies, drug dealing or whatever came from legal activities.'

'The guys we've been working for are a small part of the biggest money-laundering organisation in the world,' Ivan added, holding up the back-up drive they'd taken from the settlement. 'We've got enough information on here to send dozens of powerful people to prison.'

'That's great,' D'Angela said irritably. 'But why not wait? We can decide whether to blackmail people or go to the media when we're a thousand kilometres away.'

'Of course we will do those things when we're safe,' Pytor said. 'But Mads knows about an opportunity that would pay off instantly. It's better if he explains.'

Mads dragged his chair closer to the English-speaking group and spoke gently, with a Danish accent. 'I'm more of a hardware guy than a hacker,' he began. 'Before I was taken hostage, I worked for a German company designing and setting up electrical and mechanical systems for server farms. A few months back, Novel put a hood over my head, marched me through the forest to the nearest road, and threw me in the trunk of a car.

'We drove for an hour. When my hood got ripped off, I was in a basement. There were black bags filled with cash and shelves piled with valuables – the kind of lightweight, high-value stuff that you need to keep handy if you want to bribe a tax official or pay off a cop. Designer watches, diamond bracelets, gold ingots, high-end mobile phones. Most importantly, there was a rack with hundreds of USB sticks, preloaded with bitcoin and other cryptocurrency.'

Robin knew that virtual money worth millions could be stored on a single untraceable memory card. 'How much crypto are you talking about?' he asked excitedly.

'The sticks were labelled. One coin, ten coins, all the way up to five thousand coins,' Mads said. 'The value of cryptocurrency fluctuates all the time, but we're talking millions.'

'All totally untraceable,' Robin said, grinning wildly.

'But they took you there wearing a hood, so you don't know where it is,' Agnes pointed out.

'For once in my life I got lucky,' Mads said, smiling. 'Novel took me there because he needed an electrician to install new lights in the ceiling. I could tell from the noise there was a restaurant above me, and when I opened the fuse box to connect the new lights there was an ancient dial-up modem – the kind that people used to send data over a telephone line in the days before the internet. The unit had *Property of Mindy Burger* stamped on the plastic, along with a branch number – *1158 Locksley Transit.*'

'I've been in that Mindy Burger with my mate Alan,' Robin said. 'It's at the front of the transport plaza, where the trams to Nottingham used to start.'

'How can we break in?' Flash asked. 'They must have insane security if there's so much money in there.'

'There are two types of security,' Mads explained. 'The kind everyone thinks about is armoured doors, beefy guards and alarms with laser beams. But it's hard to build a fortress without people noticing. When you're a criminal, the best security you can get is to be discreet and store valuables in a place where nobody is likely to go looking for it.'

Flash nodded. 'Like the basement of a run-down burger joint.'

Mads nodded. 'There's steel plate and an electronic lock on the door, but the side wall I screwed the lights into is regular brick. A demolition drill could punch through in minutes.'

D'Angela wasn't keen, but saw that everyone else looked eager. 'I don't know,' she said, shaking her head and sighing. 'I lost Ivan and Pytor for six years. All I want is to get out of Sherwood Forest and be safe.'

Pytor sounded determined. 'You searched for six years, Dasha, but I was beaten and humiliated and six years of my life were *stolen*. I want to hurt those people every way I can.'

D'Angela looked at Robin, Marion and Flash. 'If you three get recognised robbing the restaurant, the Brigands will assume that you were involved in attacking their guys in the forest too.'

Flash shrugged. 'I'm prepared to take the risk for this kind of money. The Brigands have been after my gorgeous arse for months anyway.'

Marion nodded. 'It won't cause a war between the rebels and the Brigands, as long as we say we ran off and did it without Will's permission.'

'But you guys are Cut-Throat's kids,' Robin said, worried. 'What about me? Blood for blood and all that? You harm one Brigand and the whole gang comes after you . . .'

'Blood for blood is for outsiders,' Marion told Robin. 'And the first time you met my dad he gave you a set of colours and made you an honorary Brigand.'

'Does that count?' Robin asked hopefully.

Marion laughed. 'I'd keep my distance from Zoot and Insane Rob, but since you're a Brigand associate it's an internal beef. You won't have the whole gang after you.'

Ivan stood and spoke more gently. 'This was our fantasy, Dasha. It gave the three of us hope when we lay awake in our bunks at night. *One day we'll break out, rob the vault under the burger joint and rub their noses in it.* Then of course, I'd go find the woman I love.'

D'Angela laughed as Ivan swooped in and kissed her.

'I thought about you every day,' Ivan said.

Robin and Marion didn't know where to look as the kiss got more intense, but when it finally ended D'Angela had a huge smile – and tears streaking down her cheeks.

'OK, then,' she said. 'I guess we're doing a robbery before we get out of here.'

# 34. ECONOMICAL WITH THE TRUTH

D'Angela had yet to inform TwoTu that she was quitting, so she used her corporate account to summon a pair of luxury people-carriers to a layby with a couple of shops at the edge of Route 9.

This east–west road was one of the safest spots in the forest, with busy traffic and regular Forest Ranger patrols, but the two dark-suited chauffeurs still looked alarmed when their passengers stumbled out of the forest in grubby hiking gear with snow dusting their hoods.

D'Angela, Ivan, Pytor and Mads rode in the first van. Robin and Marion got plush forward-facing seats in the second vehicle, and Agnes and Flash sat facing them. The driver raised a privacy screen and as they clicked on their seat belts.

'Comfy,' Robin said, plugging his phone into a charging port as the driver waited for a gap in the traffic. 'I've even got a button to warm the seat and dry my clothes out.'

It was only four o'clock, but it got dark early this time of year. Robin stared drowsily at a sunset as kilometres rolled by. After half an hour the two vans swooped under a sign for Nottingham and Locksley, then merged onto the twelve lanes of Route 24.

Marion's sleepy state ended when Karma called. Marion thought about letting it go to voicemail, but knew that her mums always worried about her.

'Hey, Ma,' Marion said warily. Robin shifted slightly, keen to hear both sides of the call.

'We're all good here. Rescued the hostages. No injuries.'

'So, you're hiking back with Robin and Flash now?' Karma asked. 'Be careful in the dark. Bandits have been robbing people near the castle.'

Marion was too good a person to want to lie to her mum, who loved and worried about her. But she knew she'd get a blasting if she admitted that she'd agreed to take part in a dangerous robbery.

'We actually carried on north. We're all exhausted, so we're hiking to a settlement where D'Angela knows people and . . . Er, yeah . . . Like you said, it'll be safer hiking back tomorrow in daylight.'

Flash and Robin enjoyed seeing Marion squirm, and pulled faces at her.

'That's sensible, but you should have let me know earlier,' Karma said as Marion gave Flash an *up yours* gesture.

'Literally just got a phone signal,' Marion said. 'Sorry.'

'Guess I'll see you tomorrow,' Karma said. 'Keep safe and text me so I know when to expect you and Robin home.'

'Not sure when I'll get near a charger, so I'd better go now to save battery,' Marion said. She thought she was off the hook, but just as Karma said goodbye, a truck cut in front of the van and their driver blasted his horn.

'Learn to drive, you nut job!' he shouted, loud enough to be heard through the privacy screen.

'Marion, are you in a car?' Karma sounded concerned. Flash stifled a laugh.

'Yes,' Marion spluttered. 'D'Angela ordered cars for us.'

'You said you were *hiking* to a settlement.'

'I . . .' Marion spluttered. 'Look, I'm frazzled. I've been up since sunset. I said hike, but yeah, we're in a van.'

'I can smell when you and Robin are up to something,' Karma said angrily. 'Hand the phone over to D'Angela. I want to speak to her *right now*.'

'She's in the other van,' Marion said, sounding like she was lying even though she wasn't this time.

'Well, is Flash with you?'

Marion knew the chances of Flash improving the situation were zero. Since she couldn't think what to say next, she bailed.

'I think we're arriving,' Marion blurted. 'Need to put my gloves and coat on. Bye, Mum.'

'Young lady—' Karma began furiously, but Marion had ended the call.

The phone felt like hot lava as Marion dropped it into her lap and groaned.

'You handled that brilliantly,' Robin teased. Flash cracked up laughing.

'It's not funny, butt-wipes,' Marion growled, bunching her fists and staring at the sky through the fancy van's panoramic glass roof. 'I really want to do this robbery, but I *hate* lying and making Karma and Indio worry. Now they'll send me messages every five minutes and when we get home, I'll get yelled at and grounded for a billion years.'

'I'll be with you getting yelled at and grounded,' Robin said, as he put a reassuring hand on Marion's shoulder. 'But it's worth getting canned for a few weeks if we come out of this stinking rich, right?'

# 35. SO THAT'S WHY THEY PUT IT THERE

Locksley looked shabby and deserted as the two fancy people-carriers rolled through the centre of town. Most streetlights were broken, but Robin was still wary of leaving the van, knowing he'd be super recognisable wearing forest gear and carrying his bow.

Fortunately, D'Angela had spent the hour-long drive making plans, including asking the chauffeurs to make a slow drive past the transit hub.

The covered concourse where Locksley to Nottingham trams once stopped contained tents, and close to a hundred homeless people doing their best to shelter from the cold. Mindy Burger, a chicken shop and a coffee place were busy, as was the paved concourse out front where people queued for buses on the town's two remaining bus routes.

'Hopefully there'll be fewer people around later,' Robin said. 'But why are there so many cops?'

Agnes, who was staring out of the opposite window, solved the mystery. 'Locksley Central Police Station,' she said as she drummed a fingernail on the glass.

'Oh.' Robin sighed. 'I forgot that was round here.'

Flash tutted. 'What kind of idiot keeps their stash next to a police station?'

Marion tutted louder and gave her big brother a withering look. 'I wonder,' she said. 'How about a bunch of criminals who pay off corrupt local cops to keep an eye on their stash?'

Robin nodded. 'We know that nine out of ten Locksley cops are on the take, and all the senior officers are friends of Guy Gisborne. And now I think about it, who's the only criminal in this town with serious amounts of money to launder?'

Marion gasped when she saw what Robin was getting at. 'Gisborne must be working with the Russians.'

Robin nodded. 'I'll bet the bags of cash Mads saw are money from Gisborne's drug dealing.'

Flash honked with laughter. 'It's bad enough you shot Gisborne in the nuts. He'll *really* blow his stack if we rob his secret stash.'

Marion made a shushing sound and pointed at the driver behind the privacy screen. 'We need to keep our voices down.'

After their drive-by, the two swanky vans drove another kilometre and pulled into a deserted strip mall. Everything was boarded up apart from a former supermarket that was being used as a TwoTu recruiting centre, complete with bright green TwoTu signage and cardboard cut-outs of grinning uniformed TwoTu staff and slogans like WORK FOR THE WORLD'S NO. 1 RETAILER and NO APPOINTMENT NEEDED.

The place closed at five. A real TwoTu employee looked way less happy than the cardboard cut-outs as he stood in a snowy doorway waiting to give D'Angela a key.

'You've got a stack of urgent deliveries from the warehouse inside,' the employee said. 'I've arranged for someone else to unlock in the morning, so post my key through the letterbox when you're done.'

Robin waited for the employee to drive away before getting out of the van. While D'Angela switched on banks of lights and stepped inside, the chauffeurs unloaded backpacks and equipment from the cars.

Ivan and Pytor clearly remembered their espionage training, shocking Robin and Marion as they took one chauffeur out with a choke hold and the other with a tranquilliser dart.

'Someone take the feet,' Ivan said, sliding his hands under the unconscious chauffeur's armpits and starting to drag her through the snow.

Robin wasn't comfortable with the idea of drugging two innocent drivers. His face must have shown it, because D'Angela reassured him as they stepped inside.

'We need those vehicles for the getaway,' she explained, as Flash and Mads carried the second chauffeur into the recruitment centre. 'They'll just wake up with a headache. If this robbery works out, I'll make sure something nice drops into their bank accounts.'

Robin walked past a row of desks where prospective TwoTu employees got interviewed. A giant green partition separated the desks from the barren former supermarket. Its ceiling sagged from water damage and the bare floor was marked with faded outlines where shelves and checkouts once stood.

There was a coffee machine, tables and chairs where TwoTu's interviewers took their breaks, and a huge stack of TwoTu boxes. Every TwoTu box Robin had ever seen was sealed with green tape, but these had bright red tape with *Immediate Delivery* written across it.

'In the van, I tried to order everything we'd possibly need for a robbery,' D'Angela explained to the gang. 'Unfortunately, TwoTu only sells items that are legal.'

As some headed to the toilet and others began slicing open the TwoTu boxes, Robin was distracted by a text message from Karma, delivered in angry capitals:

```
THIS IS NOT A JOKE
YOU ARE THIRTEEN YEARS OLD!
CALL ME RIGHT NOW
```

'Ugh,' Robin said, trying to push the guilt out of his head.

He realised he needed to pee before doing anything else, and wound up behind Flash and Ivan in the queue for the single male toilet. By the time he got back, most of the parcels had been opened and the floor was littered with inflatable plastic packaging.

'I had to guess everyone's sizes,' D'Angela said as the group inspected the tools, bags and clothes that would stop them looking like they'd just wandered out of Sherwood Forest. 'If we need anything else, let me know. If it's in a TwoTu warehouse, I can get a drone delivery within the hour.'

Flash looked thrilled as he opened a box containing a monstrous petrol-powered demolition drill and four white construction worker helmets. Marion was less keen when Ivan handed her a plastic pack containing two pairs of sensible black shoes and two sets of school uniform.

When Marion pulled out the uniform, Robin realised it was for the super posh Nottingham Girls' Day School.

'I hate dressing up,' Robin moaned as Marion held up two grey dresses and a pair of white school tights.

'You're too famous for your own good.' Marion laughed. 'That mop of hair will look the part if we put a comb through it, and we can use the inflatable plastic packing if you want boobies.'

Before Robin could do any more complaining, D'Angela asked everyone to gather around the little tables by the coffee machine.

'OK,' she began, clapping her hands to focus attention. 'Pytor, Mads and I hammered out a rough plan for robbing the Mindy Burger basement while we were in the van. Now we need to break everything down in detail, brainstorm any potential snags, then make sure that everyone knows what their role is and has the tools they need to do it.'

# 36. MINDY BURGER MENU

Flash, Agnes and Marion made fun of Robin as he dressed up, but he made a convincing schoolgirl when he stepped out of the fancy hijacked people-carrier wearing white knee socks and a grey school dress with a puffa jacket over the top.

As Marion hopped out, Ivan opened the trunk from the driver's seat and Robin grabbed a big sports bag. It had a hockey stick poking out of one end for extra realism.

'Smells putrid in here!' Marion said, gagging as she pulled on her backpack and followed Robin under the concourse roof.

It was after nine now. The bus stops and restaurants were quieter than when they'd driven by four hours earlier, but the crowd of homeless people sheltering from bitter cold under the old tram platforms had more than doubled.

'Poor sods,' Robin said, as he walked fast with his nose buried in the arm of his jacket to stop the stink. 'No toilets, nowhere to wash.'

He felt awkward: his clothes looked too new, and it felt late for kids from Nottingham's poshest girls' school to be wandering the centre of town without an adult. But you can't get every detail perfect when you only have hours to plan a complex robbery.

A pair of cops glanced at the teenagers. One took a second glance and Robin thought she was going to ask why he was out so late, but the officer went back to hassling a homeless guy sitting on the ground. His nose was all bashed up and one broken foot was in a filthy cast.

'You think you're gonna get a night in a warm cell if you give me trouble?' the officer sneered.

The other officer tapped a long stun baton against her gloved hand. 'If you don't shift over to the tram platform with the rest of the scum, you'll get blasted with the hose they use to wash this place down.'

'Idiots,' Marion whispered. 'Why do they care where the poor guy tries to sleep?'

'Bored and like ordering people around,' Robin guessed.

They'd reached the burger bar. He pushed on the yellow burger-shaped door handle and inhaled the stale scent of Mindy Burger: cooking fat, disinfectant and customers with poor hygiene.

The three fast-food joints had been built when Locksley was a thriving industrial town and hundreds of thousands of workers had used trams to get to work. Mindy Burger's menu boards and ads were fresh, but the seats and floor had seen better days, and at this time of night most of the seating areas were cordoned off.

There was no queue at the counter. As Robin reached it he saw Agnes standing by the open serving flap at the far end. She was chatting with a manager, flirting and asking if he had any jobs available. But her real task was to count the number of staff working in the kitchen and report back.

'So, what time do you get off?' Agnes asked sweetly.

'This branch is open twenty-four-seven.' The manager sighed. 'I'm here till breakfast.'

'You girls waiting?' asked the woman behind the counter. Her name badge said *Carole*.

Robin was distracted, but he always ordered the same thing: a double chicken burger meal with onion rings and a chocolate Mindy thick shake.

'You paying together or separate?' Carole asked.

Marion stared at the menu boards as if they were algebra equations. Robin realised that the forest kid hadn't been to one of these places before.

'She'll have the same as me,' he told the server.

'Can I have a banana shake?' Marion corrected, then gave Robin a *thanks for saving me* smile.

Agnes left the restaurant as they waited for their food. When it arrived, Robin led the way to a table in a quiet area in front of a cordoned-off kids' play zone with a little slide and a ball pit. Marion ripped open her yellow Mindy Burger bag and saw the squashed, greasy burger inside.

She looked disappointed. 'That's nothing like the picture.'

'Fast food never looks like the picture,' Robin said, laughing as he stuffed hot fries in his mouth. 'You're *such* a forest kid.'

'Tastes OK, though,' Marion said, as she bit into her burger. 'And cut the snark or I'll burst one of your tits with my hunting knife.'

# 37. WALLY'S STEAK HOUSE

They had to do something to flush out the cops they'd seen around the transit plaza. Flash pointed out that Locksley police didn't come running if you crashed your car or got mugged, but you'd certainly get their attention if you damaged something belonging to Guy Gisborne.

D'Angela's career at TwoTu would end when the chauffeurs came around and reported their vehicles missing. But for a few more hours, she had high-level access to the resources of a trillion-dollar company.

While Marion and Robin ate their chicken burgers across town, a heavy-duty six-prop hexacopter drone touched down in the snow outside the TwoTu recruitment centre. It was a noisy beast, stuffed with half a million dollars' worth of cameras and sensors. It was built to fly high and collect data for making digital maps, but all that mattered to D'Angela was that it was the heaviest drone in the TwoTu fleet.

All TwoTu drones used the same navigation software. D'Angela had used smaller ones to survey areas of Sherwood Forest, so she just had to connect her tablet to the drone and program in the location of Wally's Steak House.

Flash said Wally's was an old-school steak restaurant on a prime spot by the river. It had dark wood panelling, cracked leather seating booths, and signed photos of celebrities who'd dined there back when big stars came to Locksley to play gigs.

Guy Gisborne not only owned Wally's, but he had a steak-and-lobster dinner there at least twice a week. Even when he wasn't around, lots of his crooked friends drank at the bar or played pool in the upstairs lounge.

At ninety kilometres per hour, two hundred kilos of hexacopter took a hundred seconds to travel from the recruitment centre parking lot to the riverfront steakhouse.

In the time it took Wally's diners to look out of the window and see what was making the racket overhead, D'Angela disabled the drone's anti-collision system, took it up to full speed and piloted it into the building's metal roof. It tore a hole like a bullet through a tin can and sent Gisborne's cronies diving under tables as chunks of ceiling rained down on them.

The bang was loud enough for D'Angela to hear from her spot in the car park over a kilometre away. As she jogged back into the recruitment centre, Mads was running towards her, dressed in a blue worker's overall and holding a walkie-talkie set to the Locksley police frequency.

'It's going crazy!' Mads said as the police radio blared orders for ambulances and sent every available police unit towards Wally's Steakhouse.

Looking happy, D'Angela pointed to Flash, who also wore blue overalls and had a matching hard hat on the table in front of him. 'Time for you guys to ship out.'

Back at Mindy Burger, Robin was down to his last two onion rings when Ivan texted to say that all was going to plan. Robin had already guessed, because the concourse outside was ablaze with blue lights from cop cars spilling from the police precinct across the street.

Mads had boots that fitted now, but he still got breathless keeping up with Flash on the icy one-kilometre walk from the recruitment centre to the back of the tram concourse.

'Still a couple of cops around here,' Flash told his earpiece. 'Hassling the homeless.'

Mads sounded chilled. 'I've done this a hundred times. Wear an overall and a hard hat and nobody gives you a second look.'

They went down the concrete steps at the rear of the three restaurants and scared off some rats gnawing into bags of food waste. Mads shone a torch over the sticky concrete floor until the light caught a rusting floor hatch with *Locksley Power Department* cast into the metal.

'Hold the torch,' Mads said, dropping a T-shaped rod into a slot and twisting it to unlock the hatch.

Flash jolted and almost dropped the torch when two huge rats shot out of the hole.

'You can't always tell which wire goes to which building,' Mads said thoughtfully as he studied a high-voltage junction box with three sets of cables. 'But Mindy Burger is over there so I'm pretty sure it's this one.'

Flash opened up a metal toolbox and Mads picked out an electric screwdriver. A bulb in the head of the screwdriver lit up when he tapped it against the live connector. Then Mads loosened a screw and pulled the attached wire loose, making a brief sparking sound and a blue flash.

'Is that it?' Flash asked.

Mads nodded and tapped his earpiece. 'Robin?'

'Power out,' Robin confirmed.

Robin and Marion had already dived over the back of their seats and dropped into the cordoned-off area behind them. Now, Robin crawled across the floor dragging the big bag with the hockey stick towards the kids' play area, while Marion stepped onto a chair that was mostly hidden behind a column.

While customers and staff milled around, hoping the power would come back after a few seconds, Marion unzipped her backpack and pulled out a smoke detector test spray. The device looked like a giant ice-cream cone with an aerosol can at the base. It was designed to spray a puff of smoke so that an engineer could check that a smoke alarm was working.

'I'm sorry, ladies and gentlemen,' a manager announced from behind the counter. 'I'm going to have to ask everyone to leave.'

None of the twenty or so customers seemed in any hurry to clear out until Marion released a puff of smoke and set off a deafening fire alarm.

As the manager ordered staff out of the kitchen, the woman who'd served Robin started yelling at customers. 'That's the fire alarm, folks! Head for the exits, quickly and safely.'

The restaurant had a lot of windows facing the street, so the inside wasn't completely dark. Marion hoped nobody saw her as she hopped off the chair and crawled into the play area behind Robin.

Robin glanced back and saw staff and customers exiting the restaurant. Then he shoved the bag out of sight behind some foam climbing blocks and buried himself in the ball pit.

Marion was seconds behind. Her knee thumped Robin in the back.

'Careful!' Robin warned, as the fire alarm drowned out the shifting plastic balls.

He peeked up over the edge of the ball pit as the manager checked the customer bathrooms and swung a torch around to make sure nobody was left. Then he grabbed his winter coat and a bunch of keys from a little side office before jogging towards the door.

'Thank God he's gone,' Marion gasped, putting her head above the multicoloured balls and taking a monster breath. 'I think a kid peed in here.'

Robin shuddered and nodded in agreement. 'It smells like a *lot* of kids have peed in here.'

# 38. COUNTED OUT

Marion and Robin waited a few seconds to make sure nobody would return to the restaurant, then used chairs and tables for cover as they dashed across the dining area and behind the serving counter.

While the manager stood outside the customer entrance dealing with a furious diner who wanted a refund, Robin and Marion heard messages in their earpieces.

'Sorry, can you repeat?' Marion yelled. 'Fire alarm is really loud.'

Agnes's voice came through. 'I counted nine staff, but only eight came out.'

Robin led the way past deep fat fryers and microwave ovens to the back of the restaurant, then down a tight flight of steps and into a narrow basement hallway. Boxes of food and Mindy Burger branded soft drink cups were stacked against one wall, which was broken by the doors of the staff break room and a walk-in freezer. The other side had a door with a *No Staff Admittance* sign and a fancy electronic lock.

At the far end of the basement hallway was an emergency exit, which Robin opened. Flash and Mads were on the other side.

'Jolly nice to see you, chaps,' Robin said, trying to sound like a posh butler. 'Do step inside.'

Flash and Mads had already set themselves up to start work, with a big demolition drill, protective gloves and ear defenders.

Marion looked at Robin. 'Where's your bag?' she asked.

'Crap!' Robin said, realising he'd left it upstairs by the ball pit.

'I'll get it,' Marion said, shaking her head at Robin like he was stupid.

As Marion shot back upstairs, Flash went to work with the demolition drill. He realised that he should have practised knocking something down when the hammer attachment slipped and skidded along the wall.

'Put your weight behind it,' Mads said. 'Don't let it kick.'

Flash's second attempt with the hammer was more successful, splintering the plaster and exposing the bricks beneath. Robin backed up, shielding his ears because the combo of demolition and fire alarm was deafening.

Marion stood at the top of the stairs, unzipped the bag and took out her bow and a few arrows. 'There's a lot of people out front, including a cop,' she warned. 'I'll take cover behind the counter and shout if anyone comes in.'

'Good thinking,' Robin said. He was alarmed when Marion slid the heavy sports equipment bag down the stairs rather than walking.

'My bow's in there!' he yelled furiously as Marion disappeared again.

At the bottom of the stairs the bag somersaulted and crashed into the drink cups, knocking the lightweight boxes everywhere and blocking the hallway. As Robin cleared the obstruction and opened the bag to take out his bow, Flash broke through the wall into the storage room. Now he had to make the hole big enough to get inside.

Robin felt useless watching the demolition, and wondered if he should go up to cover the front of the building with Marion. But he got distracted, first by Ivan and D'Angela arriving outside, then by a hand on his shoulder.

'Hell!' Robin yelped, spinning around and seeing a young woman in Mindy Burger uniform who'd apparently just stepped out of the staff break room.

Her name badge said *Kaia*. She had a shy childlike smile, while her short stature and upward slanting eyes made Robin suspect she had Down's syndrome, like one kid in his class at primary school.

'You're Robin Hood,' she said, sounding more quizzical than alarmed, despite the deafening noise and clouds of dust from the demolition hammer. 'I don't like going upstairs in the dark, and nobody came to get me.'

'OK . . .' Robin said, not sure how to deal with the situation and realising that even disguised as a girl, his bow made him instantly recognisable.

'Are you busting into our secret room?' Kaia asked. 'I've always wondered what was in there.'

Robin smiled. 'Maybe you should go back in the break room. We'll be gone in a few minutes.'

But Kaia was taking a phone wrapped in a case with kitten ears out of her trouser pocket.

'You're Robin Hood,' she said again. 'Can I get a selfie?'

Robin had nothing to do until the drilling stopped, so he smiled and lined up alongside Kaia.

'My favourite robberies are the ones where you dress up like a girl,' Kaia said.

As she clicked the selfie, the demolition hammer stopped suddenly, its sound replaced by the whoosh of running water.

'Bloody pipe!' Flash shouted, as Mads swore in Danish.

Robin felt water spraying his knee socks. Flash had been soaked, and so had the drill. When he picked it up, it was dead.

'Water in the motor,' Flash suggested, looking at Mads quizzically.

Mads shouted to D'Angela, who stood outside the emergency exit, while Ivan kept lookout over the covered concourse. 'Get the lump hammer out of the toolbox.'

Robin crouched down to study the hole. It needed to be bigger for an adult, but he reckoned he could squeeze through.

'I'll need a shove,' he shouted, as the screaming fire alarm mercifully timed out.

He pulled his bow and thick jacket off to make himself smaller, then popped his inflatable breasts. The water was blasting from the burst pipe and hitting the opposite wall. Robin looked away so it didn't get him in the face, but he still got soaked the instant he put his head near the hole.

Flash locked arms around Robin's waist and shoved hard. Robin's shoulder caught the jagged edge of a brick, leaving his school blouse ripped at the seam.

'God, that *hurt*,' Robin groaned, rubbing his shoulder and feeling the trickle of blood. As he stood up inside the vault, his feet splashing in three centimetres of water, the blast from the pipe turned to a tiny drizzle.

'Got the water off,' Mads announced triumphantly. 'I found the stopcock.'

'*Now* you find it!' Robin yelled furiously, his shoes squelching as he crossed the dark room feeling around until he found the electronic lock and realising that Kaia had been filming everything from the staff break room doorway.

Robin turned the latch on the inside and opened the door to let everyone in. He instinctively flipped the light switch, but with the power off nothing happened until D'Angela shone a powerful torch through the hole.

'Quality!' Robin said as he looked around.

The room was exactly how Mads had described it, filled with everything a major money-laundering operation needs to run smoothly. Five bays of shelving were lined with boxed watches, burner phones and jewellery. Black trash bags stuffed with cash stood on the soggy floor, and most precious of all were the little plastic tubs filled with USB sticks containing various denominations of cryptocurrency.

Flash beamed as he dragged the big sports equipment bag into the room. The bag contained more strong zip-up bags, which Flash, D'Angela and Robin unfurled and filled rapidly, starting with the crypto sticks and cash as Agnes relayed another message through their earpieces.

'Two fire engines arrived at the far side of the concourse. They've got to unlock a bollard and get through the onlookers, but they'll be at Mindy Burger in a couple of minutes.'

'Got that,' D'Angela replied, scooping designer watches into a bag. 'Agnes and Ivan, head to the vans and start the engines. Marion, get down here and take a bag out to the cars.'

# 39. GRAB A FIFTY

Flash threw a bag stuffed with soggy cash out to Ivan, who set off towards the two stolen people-carriers, which were parked in an alleyway a hundred metres away at the far side of the covered tram platforms.

Robin stepped out of the vault next, not bothered about the soggy jacket he'd shed, but pausing to pick up his dripping bow. He'd loaded crypto and boxed jewellery in one end of his bag, but the other end was all·cash, which was much heavier and made it awkward to balance as he leaned out of the rear door, catching the stench of human waste and restaurant garbage.

Workers who'd left the chicken shop next door when the fire alarm went off stood around at the top of the steps. As Robin shot past, they yelled encouragement and opened their phones to take video.

'Fight the power, Robin Hood!'

'Stick it to the man!'

The workers meant no harm, but the two cops who seemed to be devoting their entire careers to hassling homeless people on the tram platforms turned their heads when they heard the name of the most wanted kid in town.

The pair started to walk briskly from the far end of the crowded tram platforms as Ivan threw his bag in the back of the first van. At the same time, Agnes arrived from her lookout position around the front and settled in the driver's seat of the second.

The cops had guns, but a dozen tents and a hundred homeless people stood between Robin and the officers, and even Locksley police drew the line at shooting wildly into crowds.

Robin glanced over his shoulder and made sure nobody was coming from the other direction. He'd easily make the last sixty metres to the car before the cops got a clear shot, but the same couldn't be said for Marion, Mads, Flash and D'Angela, who were still inside Mindy Burger.

Robin stopped behind a concrete column and tapped the button to activate his earpiece microphone. 'Cops approaching from the end of the tram platforms. I'm gonna try a diversion, but you guys need to get out fast.'

'On our way, kid,' D'Angela answered.

Robin unzipped his bag, pulled out an armful of loose cash and flung it across the concourse as he yelled at the homeless folk at the end of the platform. 'Free money! Free money! I'm Robin Hood. Free money!'

As Flash sprinted up the steps with two heavy bags, almost clattering into Robin, dozens of homeless people and the dudes from the chicken shop charged in to grab cash.

'That's ours!' Flash protested, yanking the back of Robin's blouse as he threw more cash into the air.

'We've got more than enough,' Robin gasped.

As Robin ran after Flash, a gust of wind whipped twenty-, fifty- and hundred-pound notes further along the platforms and towards the frenzy of grasping homeless people. The cops shouted for them to get out of the way, but by the time Robin and Flash reached the van the cops had abandoned the chase and had started grabbing money for themselves.

Rather than waste time loading the bags in the trunk, Robin and Flash threw them in the plush passenger compartment and jumped in. Mads was last to arrive, hurling in his bag and diving on top as Ivan pushed the button to shut the side door.

'Nice distraction,' Mads told Robin cheerfully.

'Careful!' Robin yelled, pulling his bow out of the way as Mads almost trod on it.

There was no sign of cops as they turned right out of the alleyway, sped down a concrete ramp and cut through the lowest level of a multistorey car park, which was now only used by skateboarders and street artists.

As the van cut onto a deserted main road and skimmed past a burnt-out superstore, Robin looked back and saw the second car, Agnes at the wheel, closing behind them.

Robin hadn't fully zipped his bag after throwing the money around, and Flash dipped in and sifted his hands through the loose cash. 'Never seen so much money in my life!' he said. 'What do you reckon we've got? Half a million each?'

'If that cryptocurrency is worth what it says on the labels, we could net double that,' Robin said. 'I'm not sure how we'll divide watches and jewellery between eight, or how much that stuff is worth.'

Mads thought for a few seconds. 'I guess we take turns and pick what we think is most valuable.'

Cutting through the graffiti-strewn car park then four left turns had taken the two vans on an indirect route back to the TwoTu recruitment centre.

'Won't be long before the cops identify us,' D'Angela warned as she stepped out of the second vehicle.

Pytor had stayed behind, keeping an eye on the tied-up chauffeurs, listening to the police radio, and making sure that the eight brand-new electric scooters they planned to use for the next stage of their getaway were unpacked and fully charged.

'Most cops are still at Wally's Steakhouse,' Pytor said. 'But someone radioed in that you left in these two vans, so we need to divide the loot and leave here as quickly as possible.'

Flash gave Agnes a quick kiss as everyone dragged the bags of loot inside. Then he looked at Robin, who was keen to get out of the cold and swap his wet girls' school uniform for his regular clothes.

'There's an abandoned house I used when I was on the run,' Flash told Robin. 'You and Marion can stay there with Agnes and me tonight. We'll work out the safest way to get you back to Sherwood Castle with your share of the loot in the morning.'

'We'll have to be careful,' Robin said as he tugged his wet blouse over his head. 'People will hear about the robbery and know we're carrying money and . . .' He trailed off as he looked outside and realised there was nobody left in the second car.

'Where's Marion?' he shouted, loud enough to get everyone's attention.

D'Angela glanced about, confused. 'I thought she rode with you guys.'

Robin was horrified and struggled to breathe. 'Marion went upstairs to keep watch, in case anyone came in the front of the restaurant. I assumed she came out last and got in the car with you.'

Flash furiously kicked out at a desk. 'How could we leave her behind?'

Robin tapped the transmit button on his earpiece, sounding desperate. 'Marion? Marion, do you copy? Where are you?'

# 40. THAT'S WHERE SHE WENT

While Robin had been flinging stacks of money at homeless people behind Mindy Burger, Marion had been inside, peeking over the serving counter at the scene outside the main door.

Customers had given up on getting refunds and had headed off. This left seven frozen staff with nothing to put over their corporate yellow polo shirts, the manager who'd taken his coat, and onlookers who had nothing better to do while waiting for the next bus.

A fire engine arrived at a bollard designed to keep vehicles off the concourse, blue lights flashing but sirens off. As one fire officer jumped out with a key to drop the bollard, another jogged over the snowy pavement to the Mindy Burger staff at the entrance.

Marion couldn't hear the conversation between the restaurant manager and a firewoman, but their body language was calm. It was something like, *Power went out but there's no smoke. Can't be anything serious – probably just a blown fuse.*

Agnes was supposed to be keeping watch from the front concourse, so Marion was surprised she hadn't radioed a warning about the fire engines arriving. She reached up to tap the transmit button on her earpiece and was shocked to find nothing there.

After quickly checking that it wasn't in her other ear, Marion flashed her torch around the floor. The earpiece hadn't fallen anywhere nearby, and she decided it wasn't worth extending the search.

As Marion looked over the counter again, she saw three fire officers outside the entrance. It seemed they'd be stepping in soon, but they were being ultra-cautious and pulling on respirator masks.

'Time to leave, guys,' Marion shouted, crouching low as she ran back to the stairs. 'I can't find my earpiece.'

Then she heard a sound, like lots of people jostling, but couldn't figure out what was happening. Then she heard D'Angela shouting into her earpiece from the back door. 'Agnes, I've got the last bag and I'm heading out. I'll be with you in thirty seconds.'

It was much darker on the stairs than in the restaurant, where light leaked in from the street. Marion shone her torch down and was startled when she heard a gasp and saw a small, stocky Mindy Burger employee halfway up the narrow stairs. Her name badge said *Kaia*, and she looked lost and scared.

'Robin threw money and they're all fighting out back,' Kaia said.

'I need to get through,' Marion said, feeling a shot of angst as she realised that everyone else had left. 'All of the other staff are out front by the main door.'

'I hate them – they're mean to me,' Kaia said, shaking her head.

Marion could see Kaia was a vulnerable person, but could also feel her chance to escape disappearing. A fireman in a respirator was now coming through the front entrance, and it seemed that several homeless people had charged in downstairs after D'Angela had left.

'Let me by,' Marion told Kaia firmly as she squeezed past. 'Please go to the top of the stairs and the fireman will look after you.'

But when Marion reached the bottom of the stairs, three homeless men blocked the gloomy hallway and it sounded like more had piled into the vault room.

A huge guy guarded the rear door to stop more from getting in, while the ones inside the vault alternated between triumphant yelps and swearing as they fought over soggy banknotes, spilled from a rubbish sack that had disintegrated when Flash picked it up.

Marion had her bow in her pack, but shooting through a crowd of homeless folk wasn't viable. Escape seemed hopeless when someone outside tried to flatten the man blocking the back door by ramming him with a wheelie bin.

Marion realised that her only option was to bluff her way out. She doubled back up the stairs and caught up with Kaia at the top. A firewoman's powerful torch beam caught them as they reached the back of the kitchen.

'Why on earth are you still in here?' the woman demanded furiously.

Her harsh tone gave Kaia a fright, which gave Marion a chance to put a reassuring hand on Kaia's shoulder.

'She was very frightened,' Marion said soothingly. 'I'm trying to help her.'

'OK.' The firewoman nodded. 'Have you seen any smoke or fire?'

'No,' Marion said. 'But there's a bunch of crazy people fighting downstairs.'

'Both of you get out of here,' the firewoman said, pointing to the door. 'Fire can kill in seconds. The next time you hear a fire alarm, leave the building the instant you hear it.'

'Sorry,' Marion said, acting the ditsy schoolgirl as she linked arms with Kaia and headed for the entrance.

The scene out front had changed radically in the minute and a half since Marion left the counter. The cops seemed to have got the message that it was a robbery and officers spewed out of the precinct, holding shields and strapping on riot helmets.

Most jogged straight around the back to deal with the money riot, but a few lingered on the concourse and a woman in a uniform with inspector's stripes was heading towards Mindy Burger.

Marion hoped she'd pass for an innocent schoolgirl as she stepped into the cold with Kaia. The bow sticking out of her backpack was a giveaway, but Marion had darkness on her side and it would look even more suspicious if she stopped to ditch the bow in such a public place.

'Nice job looking out for Kaia,' Marion told the Mindy Burger employees scornfully. 'You should be ashamed of yourselves.'

They all looked guilty, but before the manager could make excuses for abandoning a vulnerable colleague the police inspector shouted, 'Hey! Stop!'

Marion thought she'd been recognised, but a homeless woman with dreadlocks and a hoodie stuffed with soggy money came stumbling out the front of Mindy Burger. She slipped in the snow, making it easy for the inspector to grab the back of her hoodie.

Another cop in full riot gear ran in to assist, hoisting the woman out of the snow and slamming her ruthlessly into the restaurant's glass frontage. The inspector zapped the homeless woman with a stun stick, even though she was skin and bone and had zero chance of getting away.

Marion would have loved to notch an arrow and shoot the cop in the arse, but drawing a weapon would be suicidal with so many armed officers nearby. Instead, she took the arrest as an opportunity to get away.

She didn't know central Locksley, but figured she'd put as much space as possible between herself and the robbery scene and work out where she was later.

Ice crunched underfoot as Marion walked briskly away from the concourse and cut into a deserted side street. She glanced back at her bow as she passed the collapsed awning of an old cinema. The weapon was nothing fancy, but Robin had taught her to shoot with it and she felt sad as she took it from the backpack and threw it in the deserted road.

*Should be able to afford a new one*, Marion thought as she pulled out her phone to arrange a pickup. But as she stopped walking and scrolled down to Robin's number, a single headlight beam lit up her back.

She glanced over her shoulder at a Locksley police motorbike. She thought about retrieving her bow and arrow, but it was ten metres behind her. The bike revved its engine and started towards her.

Motorbikes aren't great in icy conditions, and the rider wobbled and the back wheel spun as Marion started to run. She took a left, then a right into a narrow alleyway. The bike closed in rapidly, but Marion gained some time by knocking a dustbin into its path.

As the police rider stopped to kick the bin out of the way, Marion was surprised to exit the alleyway into a well-lit, busy street, with trendy food stalls, a uni student crowd and pounding dance music emerging from a section of abandoned tram tunnel. Hoping that the bike would lose her in the crowd, Marion dodged behind a burrito truck and a stall frying up eggs, sausage and bacon called *Breakfast for Dinner*.

A young couple almost lost their kebabs as Marion shoved her way between them. Then as she cleared the breakfast stall, an enormous brick wall of a cop came out of nowhere, tackling her so hard she was lifted half a metre off the ground.

As Marion flew backwards into the breakfast stall, strands of her long hair caught on a hot grill plate and burned. It got worse when she tried to save herself, instinctively grasping at her hair, then screaming as her fingers touched hot metal and fat on the grill.

As Marion sobbed in pain, the huge cop swept her legs away. If snow hadn't softened her landing, she might have broken something. Instead her wrists were yanked up behind her back and metal cuffs were snapped on her wrists and squeezed tight. Her burnt fingers were agony.

'Where's your boyfriend Robin now?' the giant cop snarled, yanking Marion to her feet.

Marion wasn't as famous as Robin, but her face was on wanted posters and millions had watched online videos of Marion and Robin stealing from a branch of Captain Cash.

'Let her go,' a guy with blue streaks in his hair yelled.

A few other student types shouted 'Gisborne's stooges!' and 'Pigs!', and one guy threw a sausage. But mostly people just snapped photos and took videos of Marion in cuffs.

Marion muttered a prayer, asking for the mob to rescue her or for an arrow to fly out of nowhere and spear the monster who'd cuffed her. But there were two more armed cops on the scene to keep the crowd back. The monster held on to Marion, and the motorcycle cop rolled to a stop and cut her engine.

As one officer called for a riot van to take Marion away, the motorcycle cop blew hot breath into her ear. 'You'll be all grown-up by the time they let you out of prison.'

'If Gisborne doesn't get hold of her first,' the giant holding her cuffs teased.

Marion didn't want to give the cops any satisfaction, but her burnt fingers were blistered, her cuffs were excruciatingly tight, and she was close to passing out from pain. Tears streamed down her cheeks.

# 41. #MARIONMAIDBUSTED

Robin's phone started blowing up with notifications before he'd finished putting his regular clothes back on. Most social media posts showed Marion after the arrest, but one student had filmed the moment where her fingers sizzled on the grill. It made Robin feel sick.

There was no realistic prospect of rescuing Marion, and the getaway vans would likely get spotted outside before long, so all the seven remaining robbers could do was divide the loot before going their separate ways.

'I'll do everything I can to help Marion,' D'Angela told Robin as they had a quick goodbye hug. 'And let me know if you have any trouble with the power at Sherwood Castle. I know enough about Rex Lairde's dirty dealings to make sure those lights stay on.'

'Hope we manage to stay in touch,' Robin told her, though he felt flat and distant, his emotions steamrollered by the shock of Marion's arrest.

Robin watched as D'Angela sped off on an electric scooter. Mads, Pytor and Ivan were on identical scooters behind, carrying their loot in matching black backpacks. He suspected that D'Angela had another vehicle waiting a few blocks away, but a cop can't make you give up information you don't have, so the two groups hadn't shared their getaway plans.

Flash was strong, and managed to balance his backpack on one shoulder and Marion's share on the other. Robin was on the last electric scooter to leave the snowy parking lot, trailing Flash and Agnes in a rapid convoy, sticking to storm drains and abandoned housing estates to avoid cops.

Their stop for the night was a boarded-up bungalow, soon to be consumed by the giant excavations for Guy Gisborne's latest landfill dump. Agnes's pregnancy meant she got sofa privileges. While she snored, Robin and Flash huddled together in sleeping bags in front of a propane bottle heater.

It had been an exhausting day, but neither of them slept because they were so worried about Marion. Every time Robin shut his eyes, he saw recordings of the arrest. She was feisty and funny in real life, but in the videos she looked desperate. A crying kid with a wonky leg.

At daybreak Flash phoned a friend and spent the first of his cash on a sensible six-year-old minivan. He told Robin he would head north with Agnes, use their false identity papers to register for medical care, then lie low until after the baby was born.

Robin hoped this was true, but wondered how long the volatile teenage couple could stay out of trouble, especially with so much money in their hands.

'Message me if you hear anything about Marion,' Flash said when he dropped Robin behind a deserted coffee shop, close to where Route 24 entered the forest.

Marion's arrest and CCTV footage of Robin throwing handfuls of stolen money into a scrum of homeless people had topped the morning news bulletins and was still trending online. Will Scarlock knew that every bandit in the forest would be after the loot on Robin's back, so he sent Azeem, Lyla and Ten Man out to meet him at the coffee shop and escort him back to Sherwood Castle.

'The good news is, Karma and Indio got in touch with the lawyer Tybalt Bull the instant they found out that Marion had been arrested,' Azeem explained as they jogged through the snowy forest. 'The government regard us as terrorists, and Tybalt used that to his advantage, making sure the national police got involved. They took Marion straight from having her burns treated at Locksley General Hospital to Pelican Island Juvenile Detention Centre.'

Robin gasped. 'My dad's in prison at Pelican Island. He says it's mental.'

'Certainly no holiday camp,' Lyla agreed. 'But better than a Locksley police cell where Guy Gisborne can get his hands – or his whips – on her.'

Ten Man carried all Robin's gear, but he still felt the loss of a night's sleep as Azeem sped through the forest. Robin had a throbbing headache and bricks for feet as he walked the eleven floors up to the penthouse, a loot-filled backpack over each shoulder.

Baby Zack was sleeping and the other kids were all in school, so the apartment's marble walls had a quiet, tomblike air as Robin walked into the kitchen, where he found Karma and Indio at the big dining table with mugs of half-drunk coffee.

'You look beat,' Indio said sourly as Robin stopped in front of them and let the backpacks drop.

'Sorry about Marion,' Robin said weakly. 'It's good that you got Tybalt on the case.'

Karma's lips tightened. 'What else were we going to do?'

Indio sighed. 'She's our daughter, even when she doesn't listen to us.'

After a moment of awkward silence, Robin put one of the backpacks on the table.

'This is Marion's share,' he said, unzipping the bag and showing off a stack of fifty-pound notes. 'Our shares came to about £753,000 in cash and cryptocurrency, plus whatever the dozen pieces of jewellery and designer watches we each got are worth. Ten Man used to rob jewellery stores. He knows someone who'll get the stuff valued and pay us a good price.'

Robin stopped speaking, noticing Karma's furious eyes and Indio's trembling hand.

'I'm going to give half my share to Will,' Robin said. 'It'll mean plenty of money for food, hospital supplies, schoolbooks and stuff.'

'Money,' Indio spat, picking up her phone from the table and shaking it. 'Is that what you think we should be talking about right now? How many times did we call you last night? Did you and Marion have a laugh, sitting in the back of that car ignoring my messages? I guess it worked out OK for you, Robin, but *my* daughter is going to spend the rest of her childhood behind bars.'

Robin took a step back from the table and stared down at his boots as Karma took off her reading glasses and smudged a tear out of one eye.

'Cat got your tongue?' Indio asked.

'I'm not the boss of Marion,' Robin said, barely looking up from the floor. 'I told you I was sorry.'

'Well, that solves everything,' Indio said sarcastically. 'Marion was *always* mischievous. But it used to be normal kid stuff, like coming back late from fishing trips with her cousin Freya, or lying about finishing her homework. Then you come along and she's blowing up buildings and robbing banks.'

'I didn't do any of that stuff before I met Marion,' Robin snapped back bitterly. 'So maybe she's the bad influence on me.'

Indio shot up from the table, looking like her head was about to explode. Karma stepped in front of her, calmer but still upset.

'Matt already hero-worships you and tries to copy everything you do,' Karma said. 'It'll be Finn and Otto next.'

'I've never hit a child in my life, but I'm so angry I could slap you silly right now.' Indio was sobbing. 'I sent nine messages. I begged Marion to be sensible and come home.'

'Are you gonna kick me out of here?' Robin asked, feeling sick.

'No,' Karma said, sighing. 'That's not how parenting works.'

Indio managed a slight smile. 'We're insanely angry with you right now, but we still love you.'

'We're angry at Marion too,' Karma added.

Robin tried to apologise again, but broke down in sobs. As Karma stepped around the table to give him a hug, he thought about how he might not see his best friend for years and how, for once in his life, he wished he'd done what the grown-ups had told him to . . .

# 42. ROBIN'S NEST

It was three days after Marion's arrest. The sun was starting to set as Robin stood on the roof above the Nest. Josie was half a step to his left, aiming a bow at a high-end graphics card propped on a stool ten metres away.

'It looks expensive,' Josie said. 'Are you sure it can't be repaired?'

'The Super kept frying £2,000 GPUs until D'Angela tracked down a fault in the power supply,' Robin explained. 'Now, draw back the bow string. Close one eye and hold your breath, like I showed you last time.'

Robin was close enough to see the fine hairs on Josie's neck. He gently corrected her aim as she drew back the bow.

'Do I need to correct for wind?' Josie asked.

'Not at this range.'

Josie gasped as she released the arrow, then leaped in the air as its metal tip smashed the graphics card dead centre. There was a satisfying thunk as the arrow tore between the metal ribs of the card's heat sink, sending splintered plastic in all directions before landing softly in the snow.

'Great shot,' Robin said.

'I know.' Josie beamed. 'I'm awesome!'

'It's great that you decided to drop by,' Robin said as Josie walked towards the stool to retrieve the arrow and put the remaining pieces of the graphics card back in place for another shot. 'I'm not the most popular kid in the Maid household right now.'

'Blaming you's not right,' Josie said firmly. 'Marion made her own decisions. It's sad, but she knew the risks, same as everyone else.'

'They're not being horrible or anything,' Robin clarified. 'But Marion's facing twelve years' jail time and Indio is angry with me.'

'Rough,' Josie said, giving Robin a sympathetic smile.

Robin looked down at the snow guiltily. 'If we'd just done a head count before we drove out of Mindy Burger . . .'

Robin was surprised when Josie notched an arrow and released it quickly. He expected the shot to go wide, but she speared one of the cooling fans along the side of the graphics card.

'You're a natural,' Robin said happily, then he heard a muffled shout and turned to see Matt Maid's head sticking through the roof hatch.

'I called your phone,' Matt shouted irritably. 'Karma said to tell you there's some big thing you'll want to watch on the news.'

Robin pulled his phone from his hoodie, realising that he'd left it on silent after school. 'Is Karma talking about the pictures of Rex Lairde reunited with his dogs?' he asked. 'He was on breakfast TV, trying to get sympathy by telling this whole made-up story.'

Matt shook his head as he stepped out onto the snowy rooftop. 'Sheriff Marjorie was talking to the press on TV and . . . I don't know. Something about hackers and stolen paintings. Mum told me to find you because she thought you'd want to watch it. She also said to let you know that dinner will be ready in an hour, and she washed your bedsheets, but you have to put them back on yourself.'

'What's for dinner?' Robin asked, deciding it would be rubbish trying to download and watch a video on his phone from the rooftop. He headed for the roof hatch.

'Spag and meatballs,' Matt said.

Robin slid down the ladder into the Nest, then trailed snow across the floor before sitting in front of the two huge computer screens. By the time Robin had done a search on Sheriff Marjorie and clicked to play a half-hour-old Channel Fourteen news report, Matt and Josie stood on either side of him.

'When you've finished teaching me to shoot, I'll put an arrow between her eyes,' Josie said when Sheriff Marjorie's photo came on screen, behind news reporter Lynn Hoapili.

'Harsh!' Robin said, shocked by Josie's hatred.

'My mum and sister died when their boat capsized – in a flood that evil woman caused,' Josie explained.

'God, I'm so sorry,' Robin said, shocked, and realising that he barely knew anything about his new friend.

'Terrible,' Matt added with a shudder.

The news video had kept running, with Lynn Hoapili speaking above a caption that read SHERIFF MARJORIE: ART, POWER AND CORRUPTION.

'Earlier this morning Channel Fourteen received a dossier containing several gigabytes of leaked data from a hacking group calling itself Friends of Sherwood Forest.

'Included in the dossier were videos, documents and recorded conversations which seem to prove that Sheriff of Nottingham Marjorie Kovacevic stole several valuable paintings from Sherwood Castle Resort, sold them on to a Middle Eastern art dealer then used a notorious Russian money-laundering syndicate to make the proceeds look like personal donations to her presidential campaign fund.'

'Holy pig balls!' Mat said, grinning as he slapped Robin on the back. 'Friends of Sherwood Forest? That's got to be D'Angela and the guys you rescued.'

'D-uh!' Robin agreed, slightly irritated because he was trying to listen.

The news report cut from Lynn Hoapili in the news studio to a scene of Sheriff Marjorie getting into a limousine, with cameras flashing and reporters shouting questions.

'Sheriff, did you steal millions of pounds worth of paintings and use the money to fund your presidential campaign?'

'Sheriff!' another reporter shouted, as one of Marjorie's enormous bodyguards tried to shove her out of the way. 'Can you really deny these allegations when footage has been released of your campaign staff leaving the Locksley branch of Mindy Burger pulling suitcases stuffed with cash?'

Marjorie looked furious as she ducked into the back of a limousine without making any comment. A photographer sprawled over the bonnet as her driver hit the accelerator.

'No way she can become president now,' Matt said happily, but Robin was older and more cynical.

'With all the corrupt cops and judges Marjorie owns, don't bet against her finding a way to weasel herself out of the scandal,' Robin said bitterly.

Josie nodded. 'Blame it on some assistant. Claim she didn't know a thing.'

'But it's still fun to see her squirm,' Robin said. 'And it's good to know that D'Angela and her crew are out there trying to help us.'

'I've passed on the message, now I'm off to kick a ball with the lads,' Matt said, standing up and bolting for the stairs. 'Later, losers.'

'Won't miss you,' Robin shouted after Matt, then swung the office chair around to face Josie. 'Wanna go back up top? Should be time to shoot a few more arrows before it's completely dark.'

'We could,' Josie said, taking a step back and smiling nervously. 'I definitely need to improve if I'm gonna shoot Sheriff Marjorie, but I thought the thing we did the other Friday was even more fun.'

'Thing?' Robin asked dopily, then gasped when Josie pursed her lips. 'Oh!'

'Unless you don't want to,' she said nervously. 'Sorry . . .'

'It's all good,' Robin said, gripping the arms of the chair as he wobbled to his feet, then feeling annoyed when he realised that the top of his head barely reached Josie's cheeks.

*Why do I have to be shorter than everyone?* he thought. Robin's heart pounded as he moved closer. He'd robbed banks, blown up dams, hacked computers, crashed motorbikes, shot a gangster in the privates, and starred in an online heist video with half a billion views, but the idea that he app    arently had a thing going with Josie felt weirder and scarier than all the other stuff put together.

And then they kissed.

# Look out for

# ROBIN HOOD

## BANDITS, DIRT BIKES & TRASH

# Read on for an extract . . .

# COMING NEXT . . .

Ten months after entering Sherwood Forest, Robin Hood is a thirteen-year-old outlaw. To rebel supporters, he's a hero fighting for justice, but many powerful enemies want to take Robin down.

As a new year dawns, elections are four months away and Robin's nemesis, Guy Gisborne, is favourite to be elected as the new Sheriff of Nottingham.

Outgoing Sheriff Marjorie has an even more ambitious plan: to become president of the whole country and use the army to wipe out the rebels hiding in Sherwood Forest.

But that's not all Robin has to worry about, with teachers on his back about homework, guilt about his friend **Marion Maid** getting captured, his first proper girlfriend and a massive zit on his chin . . .

# 1. ZANDER THE ZIT

Josie Longshanks and Robin Hood stood just inside the chunky wire fence that separated Sherwood Castle from its disused hunting grounds. Thunder drummed to the south and it was cold enough to see the two thirteen-year-olds' curling breath as they hacked at grass and weeds with machetes, then dumped the cuttings into a wheelie bin.

'How much more?' Josie asked, eyeing ominous clouds as she scooped up an armful of fresh-cut grass.

'Until the bin is full,' Robin said. 'You'd be amazed how much Sheila's chickens eat.'

'Those birds get treated better than us,' Josie complained.

'Until we marinade them in peri-peri sauce and eat them . . .' Robin pointed out.

Josie laughed. 'True dat.'

Her expression changed to shock as her boot caught a hole hidden by the long grass. Her jeans and the back of her heavy coat got soaked as her bum hit the damp ground.

Josie peeled wet denim away from her skin as Robin gave her a hand up. 'And now my arse is freezing!'

Josie and Robin wound up staring at each other, their noses only centimetres apart. Plumes of breath merged as Robin admired Josie's dark eyes and the tiny near-translucent hairs on her cheeks.

They'd been together for a couple of months. It wasn't super serious, but Robin still found having a girlfriend weird. It felt like he was wobbling along the tightrope to adulthood, half excited and half wanting to go back to being a kid.

Robin thought he might get a *thanks for helping me up* kiss, but Josie took him by surprise, whipping her hand up and trying to squish the zit on his chin.

'Bog off!' Robin yelped as he stumbled back, almost catching the hole that had taken Josie down.

'You've got the biggest zit I've ever seen,' Josie teased, as she playfully grabbed the hood of Robin's winter coat to stop his escape. 'As your girlfriend, I have the right to explode it.'

'Weirdo!' Robin said, as he wriggled free and bounced against the wire fence. 'Why would you want to burst someone else's zit?'

'You're practically growing a second head,' Josie said, then hooked her foot around Robin's ankle, trying to trip him. 'Since you won't let me pop it, I'm going to name it Zander.'

'Zander the Zit,' Robin said, stumbling away, smirking and remembering that his favourite thing about Josie was that she was unpredictable and always made him laugh.

As their laughter died off, they heard more thunder and a growing buzz from a quad bike approaching the castle on a track that ran parallel with the opposite side of the fence.

The main road through the forest between Route 24 and the rebels' Sherwood Castle stronghold was barricaded and heavily patrolled by police and Forest Rangers. This meant a safe journey to the castle from the nearby town of Locksley involved a lengthy detour on narrow forest tracks, before entering castle grounds from the rear and crossing an abandoned hunting zone.

'That's Marion's Aunt Lucy,' Robin said, as a quad with a huge pink box on the back skimmed by beyond the fence. 'She's made the cake for the naming ceremony.'

Robin liked Lucy and considered jogging to the gate a few hundred metres away to say hi, but the storm was closing in and Sheila would moan if they didn't return to the chicken sheds with plenty of green stuff.

'I think naming ceremonies are –' Josie began, as Robin resumed slashing at long grass.

Her opinion went unaired as a massive crash sounded nearby. Metal tore, branches cracked, then there were shouts. Three or four different voices.

'That's not good,' Robin blurted, dropping his machete and turning to look through the fence.

The trees in the hunting grounds were too dense to see far along the winding track, but a haze of dirt wafted between the bare branches.

'Has to be Lucy's quad,' Josie said, as Robin tossed her a yellow walkie-talkie.

'Use channel F and call security at the back gate,' Robin told her urgently, snatching up his bow.

The fence had been built to keep beasts like tigers and zebras inside hunting grounds where rich idiots once paid to hunt them for 'sport'. Its four metres of heavy gauge mesh were topped with Y-shaped posts that held strands of brutally sharp razor wire.

'You'll get slashed up!' Josie gasped as Robin fearlessly scaled the fence.

But he had a gift for climbing. Josie became less fearful as her boyfriend snaked his muscular shoulders between the strands of razor wire, then tore his trouser leg, before balancing boots on the taut topmost wire and making a two-footed leap into the nearest tree.

'Josie Longshanks here,' she told the walkie-talkie. 'We just heard a massive crash inside the hunting grounds. Quad bike driven by Lucy Maid. Robin has jumped the fence to investigate. But there was heaps of shouting, so I think it's a bandit trap. Over.'

A disbelieving rebel security officer came back through the walkie-talkie. 'Can't be bandits this close to the castle, Josie. But give us your exact location and we'll check it out.'

Robin made a heap of noise hurtling down between branches and out of the tree, but moved stealthily once he was on the ground. Just like the security officer Josie spoke to, Robin hadn't heard of bandits operating this deep inside Sherwood Castle grounds. But as he closed on the crash scene there was no mistaking a young man barking orders and an anguished shout of '*Hands off me!*' from Lucy Maid.

Robin kept low as he squelched across a deeply rutted track. There were boot prints and drag marks where the bandits had pulled Lucy into the trees, and Robin made a quick study of her wrecked quad bike.

Its front wheels and steering column had been ripped away from the chassis. The rest of the vehicle had flipped and smashed into a tree stump. As plastic bodywork and rotten wood splintered, it had thrown up clouds of dust and a mushroomy scent that mingled with the smell of petrol leaking from the quad.

Robin saw no blood, so Lucy must have been wearing a decent helmet. But the tree had disintegrated and it was miraculous that she hadn't been knocked out. At the far side of the track a big clump of turf and a holly bush with a length of chain tied to its stump had been ripped out of the ground.

Chain traps were a common bandit tactic: find a tight corner on a forest track, stretch a chain or rope tightly across and by the time a motorbike or quad rider sees the threat, they have no time to stop.

At the back of the quad, the big pink box had been squashed and its lid had flipped open, but Lucy had packed the cake for a bumpy ride with three layers of bubble wrap. The iced lettering on top was legible through the wrapping and Robin felt upset when he read the message:

**Happy Naming Day, Zach William Maid**

'William!' Robin gasped, practically inhaling his own tongue. 'What the . . . ?'

But baby Zach's name wasn't important while Lucy remained in danger.

He could hear the bandits in the trees less than ten metres away. Lucy was conscious and calm, using a bossy tone as she urged her captors to turn their lives around and join the rebels.

'Do you want to be part of the solution or part of the problem?' she challenged them. 'You'll be lucky to get thirty bucks for my shabby phone and silver rings. But us rebels need fit young people like you. You'll get regular food, hot showers and a private suite in the castle hotel.'

Robin crept close enough to see one bandit's outline. He wasn't far out of his teens and Robin winced as he slapped Lucy with the back of his hand and growled nastily.

'Quit yapping and pull those rings off, you dirty hippy!' he demanded. 'Else I'll chop the fingers that go with 'em.'

'I haven't taken this off in years,' Lucy whimpered, tugging desperately at a silver skull ring as Robin eyed a crack in her purple safety helmet and blood coming from a cut on the side of her neck.

It seemed there were three bandits: two stocky dirt-caked youths and an older woman wrapped in a raggedy bearskin coat who held a shotgun.

*Probably their mother*, Robin guessed.

Robin reached over one shoulder, expertly hooked four of the arrows sticking out of his backpack between fingers, then swung them over his head. The first arrow notched expertly into his bow, while the other three balanced in hand, ready to shoot in rapid succession.

*One for each bandit, and one for luck*, Robin thought, as he realised that he should take out the woman with the gun first.

Robert Muchamore's books have sold 15 million copies in over 30 countries, been translated into 24 languages and been number-one bestsellers in eight countries including the UK, France, Germany, Australia and New Zealand.

Find out more at muchamore.com

Follow Robert on Facebook and Twitter @RobertMuchamore